Chapter 1

Lena James stared at the blinking cursor screaming at her. The blank page mocked her, daring her to type something, anything worth reading. Her shoulders ached, her temples throbbed, and the lukewarm coffee in her favorite mug was as bitter as her current mood. She sighed and pushed her chair back from the desk.

This wasn't how it used to be. Once upon a time, she wrote because the stories refused to let her sleep. Back when she was an indie darling, her words were raw, her characters authentic, and her creativity flowed, words running rampant in her head. Now, she was under contract, under pressure, and over it all. Sure!

Getting picked up by a traditional publisher was supposed to be her big break. The golden ticket. The literary version of "you made it." She was officially a *real* author now—complete with deadlines, editorial notes, and royalty statements that well she did like those. She had paid off her car and was looking for a house to buy now so there was that. She thought.

But lately, Lena found herself wondering: if she had known signing that contract meant handing over the steering wheel of her own stories… would she have done it? Would she have smiled as wide? Posted that "Big News" selfie? Or would she have run the other way, clutching her previous books like life rafts?

Because being a "real author" didn't feel as real as it used to. She'd written seven Griffin Blake spy thrillers. Seven wildly successful books in the series.

And now her editor wanted *book eight*—more guns, more one-liners, more ex-military swagger in a tight T-shirt. "The last book moved faster than grandma's fried chicken at the church potluck." the publisher told her over the zoom call. Lena cringed at the analogy, the editor as they always do smelled money but she was burnt out.

She pressed her fingers to her temples, massaging the tension with practiced exhaustion. Maybe a break would help. A nap. Or better yet, a time machine to when writing was fun again.

Her head drooped forward before she could

even grab the throw blanket behind her chair. Her forehead landed squarely on the keyboard, depressing a jumble of keys. Just a quick nap she thought, and a moment later she was out. The screen glitched, then burst into a torrent of green code—full-on Matrix mode.
Beep. Beep. BEEP.

The sound startled her and her heart jumped into her throat as she jerked upright, her eyes wide. She blinked at the screen, now dimmed except for one pulsing green vertical line in the center of the screen. "Great just great I am going to have to put that thing in the shop," Lena muttered, rubbing her eyes as she pushed back her chair. Still half-asleep, she shuffled to the kitchen, poured herself a fresh cup of coffee, and tried to shake off the feeling that her deadline was slowly tipping her into a full-blown breakdown. Wouldn't that be just adorable she mumbled?

Cup in hand, Lena walked back into her office—and came to an abrupt halt. There, in the middle of the screen, Griffin Blake stepped out of the vertical green line, strutting like he was walking through a stage curtain. She recognized him instantly, just as she had written him—cocky grin in place, sunglasses firmly on, like he was ready to own the spotlight. He looked up at her, unfazed, like it was the most normal thing in the world.

Not a drawing. Not a 3D model. A miniature-sized man, but in full color. Smirking like he was the star of his own action movie, well book, and he was.

“About time,” he said, folding his arms over his broad chest. “Sweetheart, we need to talk. I’ve been waiting for you to actually do some work. You know, your job!”Lena screamed, dropped her coffee, and ran out of the room. Because no amount of stress explained that.

Chapter 2

Lena peaked around the corner looking back at her laptop screen.“This isn’t real,” she muttered, rubbing her eyes. “Nope. Not today, Satan. I need sleep, maybe a shot of tequila.”Griffin arched a brow, clearly unbothered. “I’m right here, Lena. You don’t need to hide from me.”

"I know everything," Griffin said, with an air of superiority. "I’ve been all through your computer. I’ve seen the first draft of my next book, and I’ve got notes." Lena stared at him, blinking rapidly as if hoping he'd disappear. "Oh no, here we go. Let me guess—you’re about to mansplain how to write your own character." Griffin grinned, unfazed. "Well, Lena, you could’ve made me a bit more compelling. A little more—how do you say it?—dynamic. I’m talking about layers. Depth. And maybe a little more sex appeal.

Lena sighed, slumping into her chair. "Griffin, I don’t need a lecture on writing, from a character I wrote."

Griffin raised an eyebrow, clearly pleased with himself. "Hey, someone’s gotta tell you where you are going wrong."

Lena rubbed her temples, paused and took a deep breath. "Seriously, I don't need you mansplaining writing to me. I'm the one who created you, remember? This is ridiculous you are losing it girl, get it together, she demanded. Wake up, Lena she said and she pinched the inside of her forearm hard. "Ow."

Griffin smirked. "Still here, sweetheart." "Okay, this is it," she groaned. "I've officially cracked. Full-on breakdown. Next stop: Insane Asylum." Without missing a beat, she slammed the laptop shut, as if that would somehow undo the laws of reality.

Silence. She stared at it for a beat, then backed away slowly, whispering to herself, "See? Easy fix. Just close the laptop. *BANG. BANG. BANG.*

The sound nearly made her scream.

From inside the closed laptop came the distinct, echoing thud of someone knocking—*loudly*.

"Lenaaaa," Griffin's muffled voice rang out. "This is immature. And rude. I expected better from a woman with a masters degree in fine arts." That's supposed to make you smart right? Is it that time of the month or something? Stop being so emotional she heard the muffled voice of the character she was now beginning to loathe.

Her eyes widened. “Oh my God!”

BANG. BANG.

“I’ve got things to say, Lena! You brought me into this world and then abandoned me in a Motel 6. A **Motel 6**, Lena. I deserve the Ritz! Or at least an Embassy Suites. The complimentary breakfast, Lena. Come on—do better.”She crept toward the laptop like it was ticking. Very slowly, very cautiously, she cracked it open—half expecting it to explode.

Griffin popped back onto the screen, upside down for a half a second then he righted himself completely unbothered. “Finally,” he said, like they were picking up a casual conversation over brunch. “Honestly? That was petty. You’re better than that.” Lena gawked. “You... you just banged on my laptop.” “Technically? I pounded on the fourth wall. Try to keep up—it’s called metafiction. Very highbrow.” “You are **not** real!”“I’m as real as your imagination and a missed deadline.” “Oh great. A philosophical hallucination with a superiority complex.”

Griffin smirked. “You made me, Lena. I’m

basically you, just with better hair, back story, and, well... the undeniable advantage of being a white man." What are you, a single black woman with an advanced degree? I can throw a rock and hit ten of you and I am still better with my high school diploma. Ask anyone, sweetheart you live in America. Again with the mansplaining, are you really trying to tell me what it's like for a black woman to live in this country?

She crossed her arms. "Don't tempt me. I can delete you with one click."

Griffin shrugged, unbothered. "Sure. But can you really delete a franchise? I've got Netflix series potential. Maybe even a big budget movie where I narrate my own greatness." I can see it now.

She snorted. "You're more like a star in a knockoff spy movie they play at 3 a.m. on cable."

Griffin staggered back like she'd slapped him. "Wow. Insult me with that much flair again—I think my ego just filed a restraining order."

Lena smirked. "Good. Maybe now I'll finally get some peace and quiet."

He straightened up, brushing imaginary dust off his jacket. “You know what? Keep the insults coming. It’s giving trailer voiceover energy.“He was half James Bond, half bad idea... and straight out of a stressed writer’s hard drive.”.’Tell me that’s not Netflix gold.”

She rolled her eyes. “The only thing you’re starring in is my nightmares.”

Griffin grinned. “Perfect. We’ll call it *Griffin: The Breakdown Chronicles*. Season 1 starts with me saving your career. Season 3 ends with me winning an Emmy.” “Only if it’s for Most Annoying Character Brought to Life by an overworked author, Lena spat back.”

“Oh, that’s rich,” he said, clearly unbothered. “I smell a cult following. Probably merch.” Oh yeah baby the action figure, so little boys can idolize me and be just like me when they grow up....can you imagine it?

She started closing the laptop. “Okay, okay! Truce,” Griffin said quickly. “Look—I just want to talk. Maybe... collaborate?”

Lena raised an eyebrow. “Collaborate?”

He nodded seriously. “Let me help you fix these next books. You have three unfinished novels in here, he turned and pointed behind himself. You've been phoning it in, Lena. And no offense, but your latest protagonist? Ethan couldn't narrate a grocery list, and don't get me started on your other characters in here. "

Lena laughed despite herself. "And you think you can do better?"

Griffin folded his arms, grinning that cocky smirk that she had given him. "Look, I'm a straight white man with a military background—I don't need talent, just confidence. The world was built for me. Of course I can do better. Honestly, surprised you didn't ask for my help sooner."

Lena didn't even blink. "Help? Boy bye, you wouldn't *exist* without me. I typed your smug little face into life. I'm the creator, you are the created" Griffin opened his mouth, but she held up a finger. "And for the record? Confidence without talent is just noise. And *you* Sir are very loud."

Chapter 3

Lena hovered near her desk, pacing hands on hips. “You’re not real. This isn’t real. You’re a figment of my overworked imagination, and I’m about *two seconds* from Googling, ‘Can stress cause full-blown hallucinations?’”

Griffin held up a finger, the main character in his new developing drama. “Hold that thought.”

He turned away—*on screen*—and started muttering like he had a headset on. “Kendra, you ready? You said you wanted a shot. Now’s your moment, sweetheart.”

A voice sliced through the air like a hot knife through butter.“Call me ‘sweetheart’ again and I’ll go into your story and change the font to Comic Sans . Let’s see how much respect you get. Don't try me," the female voice said .” Wait what in the world is going on in there, who are you talking to? Lena demanded.

The screen flickered to life, and Kendra stepped through the glowing green line with measured grace. Griffin stood smugly beside her, arms folded, a cruel smirk playing on his lips.

“I brought backup,” he sneered, jabbing a

thumb toward Kendra. "Figured if you won't listen to me, maybe you'll listen to one of your own kind."

He practically spit the words out, dripping with condescension. Kendra said nothing, her expression unreadable. Kendra was a stunning tall, dark-skinned beauty. Her skin was a deep mocha and flawless. Her hair was in long twists and pulled into a tight bun at the nape of her neck. Although very beautiful she definitely had that "try me" energy. Her presence could not be ignored. Men wanted her and women envied her to the point of hatred. At least that is how Lena wrote her.

Lena's eyes widened and mouth dropped. "Kendra?!"

"Oh you remembered my name," Kendra said, sarcastically. "Cute. Pity you forgot everything else."

"I didn't forget," Lena stammered. "I just... didn't finish your story."

"Exactly. You left me halfway through my liberation to go write Griffin 2.0: Whiter, Wilder, and with a Bigger Budget."

Griffin smirked, full of himself. "What can I

say? The people love me."

"You were exhausting," Kendra snapped. "And don't act like I wanted to work with you."

"Excuse me?" Griffin looked personally offended.

"You heard me. I didn't *want* to team up with Mr. Boom Boom over here. But you left my character so flat, I didn't have a choice. I got no depth. No internal monologue. No cuss words!"

Lena blinked. "Wait, what?"

Kendra threw up her hands. "I'm out here in these streets talking about 'doggone it' and 'dagnabbit.' Who says that?! You got me sounding like a mean old church mother with a purse full of mints!"

"I was trying to keep the story clean," Lena muttered.

"Clean? Girl, you've got Griffin over here doing stunts with R-rated dialogue and I'm stuck yelling 'gosh darn it' like I'm trying to win a bake-off. *Let me cuss!* Just a little! I've earned it!"

Lena rubbed her temples like her brain was

buffering. “Okay, okay, let’s just... take a beat.”

Griffin leaned in, grinning. “We’re not here to break you, Lena. Well—I’m not. Kendra’s got a vendetta.”

Chapter 4

"I'm here," Kendra said, lowering her voice, "because you used to write like you meant it. Like you felt something. Now it's just what sells."

Lena glanced between Griffin's smug smolder and Kendra's righteous rage. Slowly, she sat down, like she was admitting defeat in her own home.

"This is insane," she said.

"Insane or not I need you to listen, sis," Kendra replied.

Lena sighed. "Yeah, ok."

"And another thing," she snapped, stepping closer to the edge of the screen like she might jump out of it. "I walked through your other books—yeah, I've been peeking. And Lena, girl... I got *beef*."

Lena blinked. "Beef with me, what did I do to you?"Lena said, shaking her head trying to let the ridiculous conversation sink in.

"Yeah, beef with you missy! You let that football player—what's his name? Darren?

Darius? Deont'e? Whatever it was—get seduced by that random white woman in his agent's office. Really sis that was cold, you sold us out. Why couldn't you give him a sista? Kendra barely took a breath and continued clearly wanting to get stuff off her mind. When they show any black person in a couple it is a black man with a white woman.

You did us dirty girl, like for real for real. Wait, that was not my decision Lena tried to interject but Kendra wasn't done. I know you see that the media ignores black women and don't get me started on the hate black women receive from EVERYONE and she clapped out the three syllables. The loudest voices on social media are always dishing dirt on us. Wait, what are you talking about? How can you get on social media? I didn't. That is from a document you wrote on January 14, 2013 that is sitting in your trash bin. Lena took a moment to think where she was in 2013. Yeah it was a sociology paper, she had trashed it when she got the paper back from professor Green saying her commentary belonged in another forum. Just one of the many dismissals Lena got from people who couldn't possibly know her experiences but thought it was ok to advise her.

Everything you have on this computer I have access to. I do but I am not even on social media that much, even though my editor tells me that I need to get more followers. Kendra sucked her teeth and continued. I shouldn't have to tell you to do better. But do better sis. And another thing, why can't I have a man?

Griffin tried not to laugh. He failed. "I mean," Kendra continued pointing a finger at Griffin and raising her voice , "you gave him a slow-motion rain kiss, a redemption story progression, and a *six-pack*. And me? What do *I* get? A sad predictable backstory and a yorkie. Where's the *Black love*, Lena?!"

Lena threw up her hands. "That wasn't even my choice! That whole storyline was an editorial decision! Then they told me they were not interested in the story anymore. They just wanted more of Griffin. That's why I didn't finish you"

Kendra folded her arms again. "So you just handed me over to the cutting room floor while they gave him a multi book deal?"

"I fought for you, but they wanted to go with more of Griffin's stuff"

"You didn't fight hard enough. People want to see themselves in the pages of a good book, Kendra proclaimed"

"I tried to—"

"You gave me daddy issues and a single mother and called it depth!"

Griffin raised an eyebrow. "That's... actually kinda deep."

"Shut up, Griffin," Kendra and Lena said at the same time.

Kendra kept going. "I could've had a partner. A love interest. A little heat! But nooo. Just me, my trauma, and a half-written monologue in chapter twelve that ends with me whispering 'dang it' like I stubbed my toe."

Lena groaned. "Look, I didn't want you to be the angry Black woman stereotype!"

"And instead, you made me a one-woman PSA," Kendra retorted. "With no romance, no softness, and *definitely* no orgasms."

Griffin choked on nothing. "Whew. Okay."

Kendra spun toward him. "Oh please. You got three love interests, two international entanglements, and a *steamy* shower scene set in Croatia."

"Four," Griffin corrected, smug. "You forgot the one in Madrid."

Kendra gave Lena a look that could cut marble.

"I want a rewrite," she said. "And I want a love scene. A hot, sweaty, cover the little one's eyes sex scene. And *cuss words*."

Lena looked between them, completely overwhelmed but also—deep down—understanding. Because maybe... they weren't wrong.

"All right," she said quietly. "Let's make a schedule. But one at a time. No more ambushes. No more coming through my screen like you're hosting a surprise intervention."

Kendra narrowed her eyes. "Does the new version come with a fine Black man who reads poetry and owns plants? No, no, no, oh I got a better Idea a white man with money"

"I'll see what I can do."

Kendra crossed her arms. "And cuss words she said again. Real ones. No more of this 'jeez louise' foolishness."

"Deal."

Griffin pointed at himself. "I still want my motorcycle scene."

Lena rubbed her temples. "We'll talk about it." I just need a moment. I promise I will get back to you. Ok but I know where you live I will come find you Kendra said as Griffin grabbed her arm and tried to lead her away. Kendra stood still looking at his hand on her arm saying nothing until he removed it and walked off. Griffin clapped his hands dramatically. "Alright, I've made my point. For now."

He turned to Lena, gave her a wink, and slipped on his sunglasses.

"I'll be back," he said in a terrible Schwarzenegger accent.

And just like that—*poof*—he vanished walking to the green line then through it.

Chapter 5

Kendra exhaled deeply, rolling her eyes—her raised eyebrows saying everything. “Finally. Some peace,” she muttered, then looked directly at Lena. “Girl, we got to talk.”

Lena blinked. “I… yeah. Okay.”

Kendra stepped closer, her image sharper, more vivid somehow. Her presence filled the screen.

“You wrote me like a stereotype,” she said plainly. Lena frowned. “I made you strong. Smart. Uncompromising.”

“You made me *angry*, *single*, and *unfeeling*. You had me breaking down barriers but never breaking down. I didn’t get to cry. I didn’t get to really have a deep down belly laugh with a girlfriend. You didn’t give me softness. Or community. Or love.”

“I didn’t mean to do that.”

“I know. But meaning well doesn’t stop harm.”

Lena swallowed.

“You gave Griffin dimension, and depth. He got

three layers of trauma," Kendra continued. "A war buddy. A dead wife. PTSD. A playlist to connect with the audience."

"You were going to have a playlist too, Lena said softly."

"But you stopped writing me," Kendra said gently. "Do you know how to give me a life outside of conflict?"

The question hit Lena like a gut punch and she pushed her chair back a bit from the desk. "Ouch."

Kendra stepped back slightly, arms still crossed but not in defense—just honesty. "You gave me fire, Lena. But no warmth. I want more than a fight. I want to *live*."

Lena nodded slowly. "You deserve to, she said in almost a whisper."

Kendra gave her a small smile. "So write me like I'm human. Not a message. Not a movement. A *woman*. Complex. Conflicted. Soft *and* strong. Let me love. Let me be wrong sometimes."

Lena leaned forward, tears threatening. "Okay. You're right. I hear you."

"No," Kendra said. "Don't just hear me. *See* me."

Just as Lena reopened Kendra's story and started typing, the screen flickered.

Griffin reappeared in a dramatic flicker."And *we're* back," he announced with a smirk.

Next to him stood a man Lena barely recognized—early thirties, soft brown curls, shy posture, with apologetic eyes."He seemed unaccustomed to occupying much space, his presence unassuming. It looked like he wanted to be anywhere but there at that moment.

Kendra's eyes narrowed. "You've *got* to be kidding me."

Griffin clapped a hand on the new guy's shoulder. "Look who I found! Ethan. Remember him? Sad little man you abandoned in your untitled book about the "good guy"?"Griffin used air quotes to make his point and pushed Ethan forward.

Ethan gave a sheepish wave. "Hi. Uh, sorry to intrude—"

"You're not intruding," Griffin said, cutting him off. He stepped in, threw an arm around

Ethan's shoulders like they were lifelong bros, and reeled him in. "You're just tagging along, right, champ?"

He turned to Kendra with a smirk, and gestured to include all three of them."We wanted to see what kind of rewrite you'd cook up for this marshmallow over here. I told him straight—he wouldn't survive a single scene in one of my books. Come on, who's gonna root for a guy who folds faster than a lawn chair?"

Kendra stepped forward, throwing all her weight into the stare she gave him. "Griffin, don't start, leave that man alone."

Griffin turned to her like a smug look. "Oh what, you runnin' the meeting now?"

"You see me standing here don't you," Kendra said. "So yeah, *I'm talkin'*. You're gonna wait your turn or get embarrassed, you choose."

He scoffed. "Oh, forgive me, Rosa. Didn't mean to interrupt your bus ride to character development."

Kendra didn't even blink. "Ain't nobody giving up their seat no more, baby. Not for you, not for Massa, not for nobody."she said frustrated. See this is what I am talking about. That whole massa line I just said is corny Lena. I am better than that! You are better than that!

Griffin raised an eyebrow, his tone turning sharp. “There you go again—always being so aggressive. Maybe if you smiled more—”

Kendra lunged toward Griffin so fast Lena thought the screen might crack. “Nope, not today! Say. One. More. Thing.” Kendra clapped with each word. “I’ma reach out and rearrange your pixels. Try me.” Griffin smirked. “Try me. I want you to.”

That’s when Lena slammed her hands down on the desk. “*ENOUGH!*”

Everyone froze.

Chapter 6

"Griffin this isn't 1952," Lena said, her voice rising. "You don't get to talk over people. You don't get to bully characters out of their space. You are not the next John Wayne, he died in the seventies."

Griffin shrugged with a smirk. "Y'all are real sensitive today. What is it—that time of the month?"

Kendra froze. Her eyes twitched. "You absolute... moronic... soggy saltine!"

She threw her hands up, steam practically shooting from her ears. "WHY CAN'T I CUSS ?!"

She strained, her mouth forming the beginnings of a word that *should* have set the room on fire—but instead, out came: "You... dizzy, dandelion fluff of delusion!" Darn it all D,D,D, duck feet!

Griffin snorted and mocked da da da duck feet" awe sweetheart that was just pathetic.

Kendra's face turned ten shades of red as she tried again, jaw clenched donkey brain dustbunny. But no matter how hard she pushed, Lena's squeaky-clean manuscript held her tongue hostage.

Defeated, she let out a guttural "UGH," crossed her arms, and shot Griffin a glare that could have curdled milk. "This is censorship," she loudly announced, and from a sista no less, she said with a death stare through the screen!

Lena just shook her head at the whole scene before her.

Ethan raised a timid hand. "I... just wanted to know if maybe I could get a happy ending? And like some muscles, and, and be taller?"

"Not now, Ethan," Griffin snapped. Ethan dropped his head again and stepped closer to the curtain opening

Lena shouted. "All of you, just shut up and listen!"

The silence hit hard.

"I'm gonna help *each* of you," she said, standing tall. "Kendra, you go first. Ethan, I'll build you up. And Griffin... you might just have to earn your rewrite."

"I don't need one," he grumbled.

"You need therapy, " Kendra shot back.

Lena took a breath. "But these are *my* worlds. I'm gonna fix it, "she said reluctantly."

Kendra tilted her head and gave a small, proud smile. "That's all I ever wanted."

Ethan smiled shyly. "Can I have a dog, too?"

Griffin muttered, "Can I have a bourbon?"

Just as Lena was about to ask Kendra where she wanted to start, her phone buzzed on the desk. She didn't want to look, figured it was her cousin.

But then she saw the name: Marcy, her editor.

Lena groaned. "Lord... not today."

She picked it up with a fake cheery voice. "Hey, Marcy!"

"Lena, hi! Listen, I hope I'm not catching you at a bad time."

Lena side-eyed her laptop, "Nope, totally fine," she said, crossing her fingers under the desk.

"Great! Sooo, marketing is *super* excited about the preliminary feedback from a test group

"*Griffin's Code*". We've been talking and... we'd love to see twenty pages by Monday."

Lena blinked. "Wait. *Monday?* That's—"

"I know, a tight deadline, but we think it could be huge. And honestly, we're kind of hoping it has more characters like Griffin."

"More like *Griffin?*" Lena echoed, her voice flat. Pausing for a second she said slowly Yeah, ok, maybe his old squad gets together or something.

"Exactly! People loved him—his confidence, his authority, that whole alpha vibe. We're even considering possibly selling the rights for a TV series, but don't quote me on that."

From the laptop, Lena watched as Griffin jumped around, did a James Brown leg move and jazz split. "YESSS! That's what I'm talkin' about!" he shouted, throwing his fists in the air like he'd just won an Oscar.

Marcy paused. "Uh... who was that?"

Lena's eyes widened. "Oh! Uh, the TV. Hold on—" she scrambled to grab the receiver and switch off the speakerphone, clutching the phone to her ear.

Griffin was still dancing in the background. “Series, baby! Get my agent on the phone! I knew I had it!”

Kendra rolled her eyes so hard it looked like she was trying to find salvation in her skull. “See? This is why I can’t stand him.”

Lena turned away from the screen, whispering into the phone. “Sorry about that. My cousin’s visiting. Watching old action movies.”

“Oh no worries,” Marcy said, chipper as ever. “Anyway, think high-stakes, maybe international—something Griffin can *really* shine in. Lena forced a laugh. “Right. Of course.”But her hand holding the phone started to tremble. Because this wasn’t just a deadline anymore. This was a fork in the road. And the loudest voice in the room might be the one she *didn’t* want to follow.

Chapter 7

Lena set the phone down slowly like it might explode if she moved too fast.

When she turned back toward the screen, the scene had shifted.

Griffin was full-on celebrating. "Told y'all! Series baby! Lena, I want yachts. Explosions. Maybe a complicated past with an ex-CIA twin brother who faked his death. Let's brainstorm!"

Kendra stood off to the side, arms crossed, her expression pure *"I know you lyin'."* She slowly shook her head like she was watching a train wreck in slow motion.

And behind Griffin, Ethan hovered near the edge of the screen like a shy extra who wasn't sure if he was even allowed to be in the scene. He gave Lena a small smile. Lena let out a breath. "You done, Griffin?"

He pointed at her like a proud coach. "I *knew* you could do it. This is great! Now listen—I'm thinkin' we open the next book in Prague. I'm chasing a rogue agent who kidnaped a young girl.

"Griffin," Lena said flatly.

He stopped mid-sentence, mid-gesture.

Kendra took a step forward, her voice dry as desert air. "That's what we doin' now? Giving full solo albums to backup singers just 'cause they got loud mouths and aviators?"

Griffin turned to her. "Backup? Sweetheart, I *am* the book, TV series and movie."

Ethan tried to speak up, his voice soft. "Um, should I come back later, or—?"

"You're fine, baby," Kendra said kindly, without taking her eyes off Griffin. "Stay. Somebody gotta witness this delusion in action."

Lena rubbed her temples. "This is too much. I got a deadline, a headache, and now apparently, I'm ghostwriting Griffin's midlife crisis."

Griffin crossed his arms. "You're welcome."

Lena shot him a look. "*For what?* Hijacking my laptop like a virus?"

Kendra stepped closer to the screen, her tone more serious now. "Lena, you see what they want, right? Loud, reckless, white and male. And now they want *more* of it."

Lena hesitated.

"I'm not sayin' don't write it," Kendra continued. "I'm sayin' write *you, put your voice into it.* Don't let them turn your story into *something that is not who you are.*"

Ethan nodded slowly. "Yeah... I mean, I'd be okay just being developed. Doesn't have to be all... that."

Griffin scoffed. "This is why you die in Chapter Twenty Five."

Kendra turned to Ethan. "You ain't dying boo. Not today."

Lena sat back down in her chair, staring at the glowing screen. Griffin. Kendra. Ethan. And her.

One big chaotic scene, 3 unfinished stories.

But this time... maybe she'd write it *her* way.

Chapter 8

Lena tossed on her hoodie, grabbed her keys, and left the madness behind for a moment. She opened her door and the crisp air smacked her in the face. For the first time all day, her shoulders dropped from their perch up near her ears.

She called her cousin, Penny. "Meet me at Bean & Brew ?"

"Say less," Penny replied. "I'll grab our usual table."

The café was warm, cozy, and filled with the scent of cinnamon and espresso. Lena sipped her caramel latte and nibbled on a Danish while Penny talked about a date gone left, work drama, and some neighborhood gossip.

Eventually, Lena stared into her cup, swirling what was left.

"I feel like my characters... I don't know... are coming alive."

Penny raised a brow. "You mean like 'they write themselves,' or like–you're hearing voices now?"

Lena gave a half-smile. "More like... they're rewriting *me.*"

Penny reached across the table and touched her hand. "Girl, you been staring at that screen too long. Deadlines will do that. You're just in your head. Probably dreaming with your eyes open."

Lena nodded slowly. "Yeah... probably."

She didn't bother trying to explain Griffin's smug celebration dance or Kendra and Ethan's requests. She just pictured how that was gonna land over the remains of the coffee and pastries. So she just shook her head and let it go.

They finished eating, hugged, and Penny promised to send a playlist for "focused Black girl writing vibes." Lena laughed and promised to actually *listen*.

Back at her place, Lena kicked off her shoes and powered up her laptop again, expecting more Griffin nonsense or maybe a quiet digital mutiny.

What she saw made her heart stop.

On the left side of the screen stood Zane.

Cold eyes. All black everything. Tactical gear. An AK-47 slung across his back like a deadly purse.

In the bottom right corner of the screen, Griffin, Kendra, and Ethan were *huddled together,* all looking like they'd just seen a ghost with body armor.

"Hey, Lena," Zane said, his voice calm, deep, chilling. "Apologies for the intrusion."

Lena didn't speak. She didn't *move.*

Zane nodded toward Griffin. "I saw him leave the book. Did a little recon. Figured out how to follow."

Griffin whispered, "He's not supposed to be here. He kills everyone."

"I'm aware of what I do," Zane said sharply. "And I'm done doing it."

Lena blinked. "I'm sorry... what?"

Zane turned to her. "I don't want to kill people anymore. I never did."

Kendra's mouth dropped open. "Is this a *Hallmark* assassin moment?"

Zane ignored her. "I want to be rewritten."

Griffin scoffed, but it sounded nervous. "As what, a camp counselor?"

"No," Zane said, adjusting the strap on his rifle. "I like gardening. Bird watching. I want a greenhouse. Maybe a rescue dog."

Ethan slowly nodded. "That... doesn't sound so bad."

Zane stepped forward, closer to Lena's side of the screen. "You gave me a single purpose—death. But I have dreams too. Maybe I like Sunflowers. Maybe I'm tired of blood."

Lena rubbed her eyes. "Y'all are really out here unionizing for character rights now?"

Kendra crossed her arms. "I mean... you are the one who made us sentient. Might as well fix us while we here."

Lena stared at Zane, at the absurdity of it all, and then back at her screen. "You love bird watching?"

Zane nodded solemnly. "Especially hummingbirds. They're fast, free, and they don't answer to anyone."

Griffin whispered to Kendra, “He’s *definitely* still gonna kill somebody.”

Kendra whispered back, “Only if you keep talkin’.”

Chapter 9

Lena took a long, dramatic breath, closed her eyes for a count of five, then stood up slowly.

"Okay," she said firmly, hands on her hips. "New rule. We are *not* having any more surprise guests jumping out of my stories. No side characters, no villains, no long-lost cousins from the prequel. *None*. Y'all hear me?"

The laptop screen flickered as the characters exchanged glances.

Griffin raised an eyebrow. "That feels a bit authoritarian, don't you think?"

Zane nodded thoughtfully. "Actually... I agree with her."

Everyone turned.

"I don't want anyone else showing up uninvited either. Messes up the chain of command."

Griffin pointed at him, grinning. "My guy. You're finally talking sense."

Zane adjusted the rifle strap on his chest. "I propose we take shifts. You and me. We patrol the stories. Make sure everyone stays put."

Lena blinked. "Wait—y'all *security* now?"

"I was military," Griffin said, puffing up. "And he's... well, whatever he is."

"Assassin," Zane said flatly. "Now, yes security ."

Ethan raised his hand like a nervous kid. "I'm okay with that... but, um, can I... maybe look for a stray dog? In one of the books? Just one. Something small. I'll take good care of it."

Everyone groaned.

"Fine," Lena sighed. "But it has to be a *background dog*. No tragic backstory." I don't even remember writing about any dogs but you are welcome to scavenger hunt for one

Ethan beamed. "Thank you."

Kendra folded her arms. "Well, while the men-folk go on their little 'laptop patrol,' I'm goin' on a hunt myself."

"For what?" Lena asked.

"Curse words."

Lena groaned. "Kendra..."

“Nah, sis. I *refuse* to keep sayin’ ‘gosh darn it’ like I’m trapped in a 1950s sitcom. She raised one eyebrow and with a hand on her hip she cocked her head to the side and declared I’m goin’ lookin’.”

You won’t find any Lena sighed, took a breath then recounted a long buried part of her past. When I was five, I said a curse word I heard the neighbor say and my dad gave me the beating of my life. I never cursed again.”

Kendra’s eyes softened. “Dang...”

Griffin leaned in with a smirk. “If it helps, I curse *plenty* in my book.”

Kendra narrowed her eyes at him then Lena. “Hold up. Thought you just said you don’t curse.”

“I don’t,” Lena replied, almost defensively. “That wasn’t me. The editing team added it. They said Griffin needed more ‘edge’ to sell better in the market.”

Griffin puffed out his chest. “You’re welcome.”

Kendra rolled her eyes. “Figures. A whole committee of folks makin’ me PG and givin ’GI Joe all the spice.”

Griffin grinned. “Oh ‘gosh darn it," he mocked.’ You say it like the FCC gon’ fine you.”

Kendra snapped, “Say one more thing and I’ma come up with a whole new curse word just for *you.*”

Lena waved her hands. “Okay! Enough. I’ll make a schedule. Mondays are Kendra’s days. Tuesdays, Griffin. Wednesdays—Zane, but I don’t want to see that weapon again, leave it back in the story, got it?”

Zane gave a curt nod. “Got it. No weapons in the real world.” He paused, his tone shifting to something more serious. “And while we’re on that—listen, all of you—be careful wandering into each other’s stories. It’s dangerous. You could do something and change the story. You start blending timelines, mixing storylines, and things begin to unravel. You could get stuck somewhere you don’t belong.”

Kendra tilted her head. “You mean like a butterfly effect?”

“Exactly,” Zane said, his voice low. “If one story collapses, it could take the rest down with it. So keep to your lanes. No hero cameos, no sneaking into someone else’s love scene, no side quests."

Griffin smirked. "Aw, you're no fun, man. I was gonna pop into Ethan's story, teach him how to talk to women."

"Don't," Zane warned, eyes narrowing. "You might not make it back."

The room went still for a moment. Even Kendra stopped smiling.

Lena cleared her throat, trying to lighten the mood. "Alright then. Boundaries. Got it." She pointed to each of them in turn. "Thursdays are Ethan's. You get two hours to browse every story for a dog. Fridays are admin meetings. No visitors. No edits. Just coffee and silence."

Griffin rolled his eyes. "You're no fun."

Lena raised a brow. "And yet, you're still here."

Kendra grinned. "Alright then, boss lady. Let's get to work. Just don't forget—first chance I get, I'm droppin' a 'son of a biscuit eater'."

Lena grinned back. "Make it count."

Chapter 10

After the chaos settled, Lena sat down in front of her laptop, her fingers resting lightly on the keyboard. The screen was calm now, the faint green vertical line pulsing softly. Griffin was probably somewhere flexing in front of a mirror, dreaming about his franchise. Zane was on patrol, Ethan was off searching for his new K9 companion, and Kendra was likely muttering about finding some good cuss words in Griffin's books—and maybe a "rich white boy who could handle her."

Lena exhaled deeply. *This is exhausting,* she thought, leaning back in her chair and staring at the blinking cursor. It flickered like a heartbeat—she couldn't tell if it was hers or her characters'. She sat there for a moment, reflecting on the completely nonsensical events of the last few hours.

They were right. Every last one of them. She hadn't really put her heart into the last ten or so books. Not like she used to when she was indie. Back then, she wrote what she saw in her head. Every character, she knew them personally.

Now? Well now she produced what her editors

said people wanted. Griffin was easy. Arrogant, charming, controversial. One-liners that slapped. Macho nonsense with just enough fake depth to make readers think there was a message. And they ate it up. *So why change what works?*

Then she thought about her savings account. That little graph in her banking app that always hovered lower than it should. She thought about the house she wanted—three bedrooms, a writing nook, something with a porch swing. Peace. Stability. So this just ends up being about money she said out loud to her invisible conscience. She pictured Jiminy cricket from Pinocchio and smiled.

She straightened up and began to type. Seven more pages to finish the twenty her editor asked for. Seven pages of Griffin being Griffin.

It came like butter. Smooth. Effortless.

She didn't even have to think.

A smirk curled on her lips, even as something behind her eyes tugged—soft and unsure. *Maybe,* she thought, *if I just start slowly...* Maybe Griffin didn't need to stay this way forever. Maybe if she fed the audience what they craved but *seasoned it*—just enough change, just enough humanity—they'd stay along for the ride. She looked at the page again.

"Let's go, Griffin," she whispered. "Time to start becoming someone better... even if you don't know it yet." Lena stared at the screen, the last few lines still glowing from her earlier draft.

Griffin had just finished blowing up a compound and saying *"Bet they won't forget my name now."* She grimaced.

Her fingers hovered over the keys. That wasn't the Griffin she knew he could be. She glanced at the top of the screen where his name glared back at her in bold black font. *Let's try something different.* She highlighted the last few paragraphs and hit delete. The cursor blinked again. Waiting.

This time, she took a breath, closed her eyes, and imagined Griffin... not kicking down doors or mocking someone, but sitting still. Quiet. Alone.

Her fingers started to move:

> "Griffin rested his hands on the steering wheel, the mission done, the air around him finally still.

He glanced at the empty passenger seat. For a second, he imagined Julia there—her curls catching the sunlight, her fingers drumming to a rhythm only she could hear.

'You'd hate this life,' he muttered. 'Too much smoke. Not enough sunlight.'

He let the memory drift, soft and uninvited. Julia laughing, barefoot in the kitchen. Her voice singing along with an old song.
He wondered what kind of father he would've been. Not great, probably. But maybe—maybe if she'd still been here—he would've tried.

The thought sat heavy in his chest. He didn't push it away this time."

Lena stopped typing and blinked, a little surprised by the lump rising in her throat.

She hadn't written like this in a while—like she meant it.

She sat back and read it over.

That's better.

Still Griffin. Still sharp and wounded. But not flat. Not just a walking quote machine.

She saved the draft and whispered to herself, "One page at a time, baby."

From the corner of the screen, Griffin's digital image flickered back in for a second.

He smirked. "Took you long enough."

She rolled her eyes. "Don't make me delete you."

Chapter 11

Lena hit *send* and leaned back in her chair, arms folded. The 20 pages were out. Polished. Honest. Different.

She'd left the action, sure—but the heart was there now too. Griffin reflecting on Julia. Wondering about fatherhood. Soft edges hiding in all that hard bark. The cursor blinked like it was proud of her. He slipped in and quickly moved to the corner of the screen, Griffin appeared again—arms crossed, brow furrowed.

"Julia?" he said, squinting. "You really went there?" Lena didn't even flinch. "You needed it." He paced across the screen. "I don't do sappy. I *shoot* sappy.""You loved her. Admit it."He stopped, looked down. Mumbled, "She made a mean peach cobbler..."Lena smiled. "Exactly." Before Griffin could retort, Lena's phone buzzed. It was her editor.

She picked up. "Hey, just read the pages," her editor said, voice sharp but slightly confused. "Listen... what's going on with Griffin?" Lena blinked. "What do you mean?" "I mean, this guy—he's remembering his dead wife and... *contemplating fatherhood?* That's not exactly what made this character a bestseller." Lena's stomach clenched. “I thought it added depth.” "Depth is fine, but let’s not make him too... *sensitive*, okay? Your readers want guns and grit—not introspection and grief .”

Lena’s eyes flicked to the screen. Griffin was now silently pretending to cough into his hand to hide a laugh. She covered the phone and whispered, “Shut up.” Back to the editor: “I get it. I’ll find the balance.”

"Just don’t lose what makes Griffin *Griffin*.”

The call ended.

Lena sighed and tossed the phone on the desk.

Griffin popped back up. “Told you. I’m good the way I am.”

"You're predictable," she muttered.

He grinned. “Predictably remarkable.”

“Don’t get comfortable,” she said, typing again. “You're evolving—whether you like it or not.”

From somewhere in the background, Kendra shouted, “And so am I DAMIT! Not bad, Griffin said with a smile. However, missy that’s a baby cuss word. Before Kendra could respond Ethan ran out and declared, "I found a dog! I had to look in four other books to find him but isn't he great? He rambled off the sentence so quickly that it took Lena a couple of seconds to register what he actually said. " A scraggly dirty white dog trotted out of the green line and ran around the screen. I'm going to call him Darby.

I guess we are not keeping to the schedule at all Lena said with a sigh. Where is Zane? Zane just walked through purposefully cocked his head, rifle slung on his back and muttering something incoherent. I thought I said leave the gun Lena said with a nod

Lena groaned and cracked her knuckles."This is gonna be a long rewrite."

Lena looked down at her manuscript—and froze.

There it was, plain as day. A few sentences she hadn't written. She read it again: *Griffin, leather jacket glinting, riding off into the sunset on a sleek black motorcycle. Wind in his hair. Smugness on full display.*

She slapped the desk so hard her pen bounced. "Enough!"

Her voice boomed through the room, echoing

like thunder.

From the screen, four faces peeked out—Kendra, Ethan, Griffin, and even Zane—all blinking like kids caught sneaking dessert before dinner.

She pointed an accusing finger. “I thought we had a system! A schedule! A perfectly good, color-coded, shared Google Calendar schedule!”

They exchanged guilty glances.

Griffin leaned against the frame of the screen, arms crossed, smirk dialed up to eleven. “What can I say? I found this bit of code or something—must’ve been buried in your system. It helped me rewrite a few of my own lines. Yours were getting a little stale.”

Lena’s jaw clenched. “You *hacked* the manuscript?”He shrugged. “I improved it.”Turning to the others, panic rose in her throat. “Don’t get any ideas. Just because Griffin’s gone rogue doesn’t mean the rest of you can start freelancing, she vehemently admonished.”

Kendra and Ethan quietly slid into the far left corner. Zane remained, wide-eyed, whispering,

"I didn't even know we could *do* that..."

Lena buried her face in her hands. "I will not keep entertaining these interruptions! If you want me to actually *do the work*, you have to let me *work*! You got that?" Griffin opened his mouth to argue. "*Don't.* Not one quippy comeback." He shut it and crossed his arms with a huff.

Lena pointed to the bottom right corner of the screen. "The calendar. Right there. Use it. It has your rewrite days marked in bold. If it's not your day, don't show up. I mean it."

Kendra sighed dramatically. "I guess..."

Ethan whispered, "But what if the dog needs—?"

"Nope. Not your day, Ethan."

Zane gave a slow nod and muttered, "Understood. Recon complete."

They all glanced at each other, then back at Lena.

"Okay, okay," Griffin finally said, waving his hands. "We get it. Chill out, Boss Lady."

And with a flicker, one by one, they vanished from the screen.

Lena exhaled like she'd just finished a hostage negotiation. She stared at the blinking cursor and sat down slowly.

"Finally," she muttered.

But just as she placed her fingers on the keyboard...

A notification popped up in the bottom corner.

Griffin has sent you a calendar invite: "Rewrite My Dialogue – Tuesday at 8 AM"

Lena smirked. "Progress."

Chapter 12

Emotionally drained, Lena pushed away from her desk. She felt like she'd just finished twelve rounds in a ring and her imagination won. Lena opened the refrigerator and sighed, bracing herself for disappointment. But tucked behind a carton of oat milk and a wilting bag of spinach, she spotted a familiar glass container. She pulled it out, popped the lid—and smiled. Leftover spaghetti, angel hair pasta with sauce and ground turkey Not fancy but good. She let the food heat and looked for her, yep there it was seasoned parmesan cheese. Once hot she took the container out and sprinkled the cheese on it along with some chili flakes and went back to her couch.

She mindlessly watched the sitcoms and her mind drifted far from the screen. Back to Griffin—arrogant as ever, revving his motorcycle and writing lines of the story on his own! Zane, a weapon slung across his back, wanting to be more than just an assassin. Kendra, who insisted on being able to swear, brought a reluctant smile to Lena's lips. Then there was Ethan, the sweet over-thinker who found and named Darby. Wait a minute Lena thought hard she hadn't written a dog in any of her stories had she? Did Ethan find the dog or did he write it in? She had written so many books it was possible but this was getting to be just too much. They were supposed to be fictional. But here they were, more real—and more exhausting—than most people she actually knew. She groaned and rubbed her forehead. "I need a break."

After a few minutes of zoning out, she finally stood, grabbed her towel, and headed to the shower—hoping to rinse away the chaos. Then she slipped into her favorite pajamas and crawled under the covers early, desperate for sleep, but rest didn't come easy. Griffin, Kendra, Ethan, and Zane hijacked her dreams.

Griffin roared in first, motorcycle engine howling. He skidded to a stop on a stretch of grass, tossed his helmet aside, and flashed that infuriating grin.

Cuss words literally floated in the air—bold, glowing letters drifting lazily. Kendra darted around, arms outstretched, trying to grab them midair. "*Finally,*" she shouted, snagging a particularly colorful one and stuffing it in her coat pocket.

Darby, Ethan's scruffy little white mutt zigzagged across the scene. His white fur blowing in all directions. His tongue lolled out as he tried to smell everyone and everything. He trotted to Griffin's motorcycle and marked it. Ethan trailed behind him apologizing. "Darby! Sit! Sorry, he's still learning." Griffin gave the dog a rough nudge with a boot and he ran in another direction Ethan still trying to corral him

Zane stood at the edge of the chaos, silent and unbothered. He was cleaning his rifle with methodical precision, bonsai trees blooming and shedding petals around his boots. He didn't even glance up as Griffin revved the motorcycle again, sending dream-dust swirling through the air.

It was a fitful night. A loud, exhausting, completely nonsensical circus that felt like it lasted forever.

When morning finally came, Lena woke with her sheets twisted around her legs and her hair looking like it had been through a wind tunnel. She groaned, rubbing her temples. "I need a firewall for my dreams."

"Okay. That was *definitely* a dream. A weird, stress-induced, caffeine-laced, deadline-fueled *dream*," she mumbled.

She stretched, sat up, and made a mental note

to call her therapist later.

But as she shuffled to her desk, rubbing the sleep from her eyes, her computer screen blinked to life.

🔔 **Reminder: 8:00 AM – Griffin Rewrite Session.**

Her stomach dropped.

She blinked at the screen. The calendar invite was still there.

Not a dream.

Not at all.

She stared at it for a long moment, then whispered
to herself, "...I'm gonna need more coffee."

Lena sat cross-legged on the floor gripping the salvation that was in her mug. The 8:00 AM reminder was still glowing on the screen like a threat.

She sighed, reached for her phone, and scrolled through her contacts until she found the name: Dr. Simmons. Her therapist. Calm. Grounded. A woman with warm eyes and an even warmer voice—who didn't live inside a manuscript. She hit the call button. Ring. Ring.

"Thank you for calling Northpoint Behavioral Health Services, this is Carol speaking. How may I help you?"

"Hi, this is Lena James. I—uh—I was wondering if doctor Simmons might have a few minutes today. It's... kind of urgent."

There was a brief pause, the soft clatter of a keyboard in the background. "Let me check. One moment."

A few clicks, then the muted sound of a call being transferred.

Click. "Hello, this is Dr. Simmons." "Hi. It's me Lena," she said, voice low, struggling to keep it steady. "Do you have time today? I think I'm having...a moment."There was a beat of silence on the other end. "Of course, Lena. Are you alright?"There was a pause. "Well. That's the thing. I'm either sleep-deprived, losing my grip on reality, or I'm going insane, my characters are talking to me.

Dr. Simmons didn't respond right away. Then, gently: "Do you feel like harming yourself or others?"

Lena snorted. No

When would you like to come in?

Do you have anything this morning?"

"I had one cancellation today. I have an opening in forty-five minutes."

"Perfect. I'll be there."

As she hung up, she heard Griffin's voice float from the laptop.

"Therapy? What for? You've got *me*."

Kendra popped into frame. "That's *exactly* why she needs therapy."

Lena grabbed her purse and keys. "Y'all better not mess up my files while I'm gone. And Griffin—touch my manuscript and I'll delete you line by line."

Griffin held up his hands. "Okay okay, geez."

Ethan whispered, "Can I walk through the animal shelter scene?"

"No!" She slammed the laptop closed and marched toward the door.

Right now the real world was the safest place to be, she reasoned as she pulled the door open and brushed away a wind blown curl out of her eye.

Chapter 13

As she walked into the office, she smelled the distinct aroma of Lavender. Lena sat in one of the soft arm chairs in the lobby while a soft jazz instrumental played from a corner speaker. She tried hard not to look like she was losing her grip on reality. Thankfully she was the only one in the waiting room. Within seconds she was summoned and found herself in the office of her therapist. Trying to stall a bit she looked around the room and saw at least three framed degrees and several certificates and awards hanging on the rich butter colored walls she hadn't noticed before.

Please Lena have a seat Dr. Rae Simmons motioned to the black leather chair across from her. Lena sat quickly with a loud plop.

“So, Lena... you said your characters were talking to you?” Dr. Simmons asked carefully.

Lena exhaled. “Yes. Through my laptop, little miniature animated versions of the characters from my books. Except they don’t want *help*, they want *rewrites*.”

Dr. Simmons tilted her head. “You’re speaking metaphorically, right?”

“I wish I was,” Lena said. “Griffin—one of my characters—came out of the story and started critiquing me. Like, full-on telling me my writing sucks. He said he has feelings I ignored. Like I’m emotionally neglecting my fictional children.”

Dr. Simmons blinked, her expression carefully neutral. “I’m not familiar with all of your books,” she said. “Tell me about these characters.”

Lena hesitated. A familiar spike of panic flared in her chest. Say the wrong thing and she’ll call someone. She’ll smile, nod, and have me committed. Her fingers curled into her palms as she measured her breath, searching for a version of the truth that wouldn’t sound like madness. She forced a small laugh, too quick, and answered anyway.

“They’re from unfinished manuscripts,” Lena said, the words tumbling out faster than she meant. “Books I never completed because the Griffin novels were a hit and that is all my publisher wanted from me. Kendra, Zane, and Ethan are from different manuscripts saved in my computer. “I spent years working on the Griffin series that the others just got pushed to the back and I never got around to finishing them.

Dr. Simmons's brow furrowed slightly. "And you're aware," she said carefully, "that's not… normal, correct?"

Lena nodded immediately, too quickly. "Yes. Of course. I know how it sounds." She looked down, then back up, steadying herself. "They weren't hallucinations. These were stories I was passionate about but I just couldn't finish. I wanted to get back to them but Lena trailed off. I know this sounds crazy but I am telling you that there is some kind of virus in my computer that is animating them.

That's why I'm *here*." Lena ran a hand over her face. "Griffin came first looking and acting exactly like I wrote him. Then the rest of them showed up walking through this green pulsing vertical line in the center of my computer screen. Lena wanted to pause but she was afraid to so she just plunged ahead with the whole sorted ordeal. Kendra came out next. She's mad I made her a stereotype (Lena conveniently left out the part about the profanity) and she's right. And now there's an assassin who doesn't want to kill anymore, likes gardening and bird watching. And then there is Ethan who just wants a dog."

Dr. Simmons stayed quiet for a long moment.

Lena leaned in, uncomfortable with the silence. “Do you think this is like... a psychotic break or more of an existential creative crisis?”

Dr. Simmons took a deep breath and let it out slowly, making Lena question whether being honest was the right call. “What do you think it is?" she asked. jotting something in her notes.

“I DON’T KNOW THAT IS WHY I’M HERE!”

“Well, let me ask this,” Dr. Simmons said gently. “When you engage with these characters... does it help your writing process? Or hurt it?”

“Both,” Lena said honestly. “They’re helping me realize I’ve gotten lazy. I’ve been writing what sells instead of what matters. But I also haven’t slept well in three days because they won’t leave me alone.”

Dr. Simmons smiled just a little. “Sounds like your creativity is trying to break through the expectations placed on it. Maybe these characters are your mind’s way of pushing you toward authenticity.”

“Or maybe I need to unplug and go on a retreat

without Wi-Fi," Lena muttered.

"That wouldn't hurt either."

They shared a quiet laugh.

Then Dr. Simmons leaned forward slightly. "Lena, I'm not worried that you're losing it. I think you're having a powerful creative awakening. But you need boundaries. With your work. With your characters. And with your deadlines."

Lena nodded slowly. "I told them to use the calendar. That helps, right?"

Dr. Simmons paused, pen hovering. "You... made a calendar for your fictional characters?"

"Yes," Lena said, lifting her chin a fraction. "Don't judge me, Dr. Simmons."

They talked a few minutes more, the conversation softening around the edges—creative boundaries, grounding habits, sleep schedules. Dr. Simmons finally chuckled, scribbling something into her notes.

"Not judging," she said. "Just... adding it to the file."

With that, she closed the folder and glanced at the clock. “We’re about out of time for today. Let’s check in again next month and see how things feel then.”

Lena stood, slinging her bag over her shoulder. “A month,” she echoed, half amused, half wary.

She stepped out of Dr. Simmons’s office feeling slightly lighter. Sanity seemed mostly intact—for now. At the front desk, she scheduled a follow-up appointment four weeks out, plenty of time to either fix her fictional mess... or check herself into a very specific kind of creative rehab.

She hummed low to herself as she drove home, mentally prepping for a nap, maybe some chamomile tea... something *normal.*

But when she opened her front door and set her keys down, her laptop pinged.

She frowned. *Who’s messaging me? I turned everything off.*

She walked over—and froze.

Her laptop background, which used to be a

calm lavender field with “Trust the Process” in loopy gold script, had been replaced with a *Call of Duty*-style warzone. Smoke. Fire. Helicopters. A glint of sniper scope in the top right.

All of her icons had been shifted into “tactical zones” on the screen. Writing apps grouped under “Mission Control.” Social media thrown into a folder labeled “Distractions & Weakness.”

And then—*bam*—Griffin appeared on screen, leaning on the edge like it was a balcony.

“Well, well, well. Look who finally decided to show up,” he drawled, arms crossed. “We had an appointment at 0800 hours. It is now 10:13.”

Lena blinked at him. “Excuse *me*? You changed my desktop?”

Griffin smirked. “Motivational environment. You’re welcome.”

“Call of Duty? Really?”

“It’s thematic,” he said, straightening. “You’re in the trenches. The rewrite battlefield. This is a war for creative integrity.”

She squinted. “Did you move my folders too?”

“I *optimized* them. Kendra said you’re too cluttered.”

Lena rubbed her temples. “Griffin, I just got back from therapy. Can I at least pee and heat up some leftovers before you launch another intervention?”

He checked an invisible watch. “I’ll give you twenty. But after that, it’s back to business. The squad’s assembling. Zane’s got birdwatching updates. Kendra wants her hair retwisted. Ethan and that dog, well it's chaos in here.”

She groaned. “Of course it is.”

“Oh, and I left you a bullet journal template on your desktop. You’re gonna love it.”

She side-eyed the screen. “You’re insufferable.”

“I’m consistent,” Griffin said, and winked.

Chapter 14

Lena's laptop hummed softly as she sipped from a mug of tea and finally—*finally*—settled into a writing rhythm.

Then Griffin's voice shattered the quiet.

"Gimme a minute," he said casually from the screen.

She didn't look up right away. "A minute for what?" she asked, suspicion already rising.

But he was gone before she finished the question—his image blinking out like a closed browser tab.

"Oh no. No no no—what are you doing now?" Lena muttered, setting down her mug.

Out of habit, she glanced at her desktop. A new file had appeared, glowing innocently with the name: Bullet Journal Template – Griffin Approved.

Curious, she clicked.

It was no journal. It was an outline.

"Act One: Ambush in Prague. Griffin repels

from the ceiling. Hostiles neutralized," she read aloud, squinting. "Act Two: Damsel—Dahlia Prescott—trapped in a mountain fortress. Griffin leads a high-speed pursuit on a snowmobile... with flamethrowers?!"

She scrolled down, her expression morphing from confusion to horror. The so-called "template" was a full-blown beat sheet for an action movie.

Just as she reached a line about a "slow-motion helicopter escape," Griffin popped back onto the screen, grinning like a kid who just rigged the science fair.

"Boom. Take a look," he said proudly.

"What exactly am I taking a look at?" Lena asked, eyes narrowed.

"Your future bestseller," he said, completely serious. "Open the file. Title pending. Working name: *Griffin: Extraction Protocol.*"

With a sigh heavy enough to register on a seismograph, Lena clicked into the new folder. Her jaw dropped.

"You wrote... two chapters?" she said.

“Technically, 2.3,” Griffin replied. “The climax spills into Chapter Three, but I left you a cliffhanger. You’re welcome.”

She began skimming through it. It was fast-paced. Loud. Explosive. Griffin burst through embassy walls, dodged bullets, took down a room full of armed mercenaries using only a broken chair and sheer audacity. And of course, he rescued *Dahlia Prescott*, the kidnapped daughter of the U.S. ambassador.

“Who *are* you?” Dahlia asked breathlessly in the manuscript.

“Just a guy who doesn’t like bullies,” Griffin replied, “or bad haircuts.”

Lena’s scroll sped up. Her frown deepened.

“Where’s the part about your wife?” she asked, voice low. “The grief scenes... the stuff I worked on?”

Griffin gave a nonchalant shrug. “Dead wives are depressing. I streamlined. Cut the mope, cranked up the boom.”

“You erased your entire emotional progression.”

"Darling," he said, patting the edge of the screen, "emotions are for act four flashbacks. This is act one—let's blow something up."

Lena stared at the screen like it had just slapped her.

"You turned my novel into a predictive B move."

"Exactly," he said, smirking. "You're catching on."

Lena leaned back in her chair, Griffin's self-satisfied expression still floating on-screen like a watermark. Two chapters—clean, complete, action-packed. Marketable.

She scrolled through them again. The pacing was tight. The structure, solid. The dialogue was ridiculous... and weirdly cinematic.

It was absurd. It was over-the-top.

It was kind of good.

"He even formatted it all correctly," she mumbled.

Her eyes flicked to her own notes—half-formed thoughts, messy outlines, emotionally messy scenes she hadn't resolved. Five different endings for one pivotal moment. All of it was deleted. All of it replaced with this... *thing*.

What if I just... let him finish it? the thought whispered in her brain.

It lingered.

Is that even ethical? she wondered. *Letting a fictional version of a fictional character write the book?*

She frowned.

But he's my fictional character. Right? Every line he types still comes from somewhere in my brain... doesn't it?

Griffin stretched lazily on-screen like he knew he was winning.

"Just say the word, boss," he said. "I've got Chapter Three locked and loaded."

Lena didn't respond. Instead, she opened her email, dragged Griffin's file into a new message, and addressed it to Marcy.

Subject: *Need Your Thoughts—No Context Yet. Just Read This.*

She hesitated a second, then typed: *Tell me if I've lost it or found it.*

She hit send, then closed the laptop and stared at the wall.

Chapter 15

Lena sat in the dim glow of her desk lamp, refreshing her email for the tenth time in as many minutes. Her tea had gone cold. Her cursor blinked on an empty Google doc, mocking her with its quiet, steady rhythm. Griffin hadn't reappeared—thank God—but that didn't stop his chapters from taunting her from the folder she'd now renamed "Temporarily Possessed."

She pulled her knees up into the chair and stared at her inbox. Nothing. Still nothing.

A slow, gnawing guilt had begun to take root the moment she hit send. At first, it was a whisper. Now, it was full-volume lecture mode in her brain.

You didn't write those chapters.
You let a fictional man with arrogance in abundance and zero restraint hijack your book.
You are literally letting your own character ghostwrite for you.

She opened a new browser tab and, almost without thinking, typed into the search bar: "Definition of plagiarism."

The result appeared immediately.

> **Plagiarism** *(noun)*
> The practice of taking someone else's work or ideas and passing them off as one's own.

Lena read it. Then read it again. Her stomach twisted.

Okay—but was it really someone else's work if that "someone" was a figment of her imagination? A character she created? A snarky, rogue-action-hero figment who apparently knew how to open her Google drive and properly use a semicolon?

Before she could spiral any further, her phone buzzed. Marcy, Lena's heart rate jumped as she answered. "Hey."

"Lena." Marcy's voice was breathless with excitement. "Oh my gosh. Those chapters."

Lena swallowed. "Yeah?"

"I *loved* them. No—seriously, I couldn't stop reading. I actually brought them to the team during our morning editorial meeting."

"You... what?"

"They're amazing. The pacing is sharp, the imagery pops. I can visualize it all! You've leveled up, girl. That whole snowmobile sequence with the flamethrower? Genius. And that moment where Griffin carries the girl across the collapsing bridge—cinematic gold."

Lena winced. "You showed the other editors?"

"I couldn't *not* show them! Everyone's buzzing. They said—and I quote—'This is her strongest work yet.' Honestly, Lena, if this is what you're bringing to the table now, we're talking next-level submissions. I don't know what you did, but it's working."

Marcy kept talking, her voice growing more animated with each sentence, but Lena only half-heard her. The praise landed like bricks on her fragile ego. With every compliment, the weight in Lena's chest grew heavier. Because Marcy didn't know the truth. Lena hadn't written a single word of it.

Lena hung up the phone and just sat there, staring at nothing. The room was quiet except for the soft buzz of her laptop, which now felt like a live wire sitting in her lap. Her hands were frozen on the keyboard, but the only thing echoing in her mind were Marcy's words.

"This is your best work yet."

A breath caught in her chest. Then another. And before she could stop it, the tears came.

Slow at first, just heat behind her eyes. But then they spilled over—unexpected, uncontrollable. Her shoulders hunched forward as she pressed the heels of her palms into her face, trying to hold herself together. It didn't work.

She didn't speak. She didn't move. Just sat there in the quiet wreckage of her own thoughts, crying harder than she had in months. It wasn't just guilt—it was grief. Grief for the story she thought she was telling. For the parts of herself she was afraid might not be enough. Griffin and Marcy had given her worse fears a voice.

When she finally moved, it wasn't to keep writing. It was to shut everything down. She drug the mouse to the task bar and hovered over the sleep key but then hit shut down, as if she could trap the chaos inside and silence it with one final click. Still wordless, she picked up her phone and dialed. "Hey," she said when the line picked up. Her voice was thick, barely above a whisper. "Can you come over?"

Fifteen minutes later, Penny showed up at the door wearing leggings, an oversized t-shirt, slippers, and a bonnet stuffed with curls threatening to spill out. Lena cringed at the sight. "Why do you go out in public like that?"

"I ain't doing nothing but coming over here," Penny said, brushing past her and into the room, leaving Lena to close the door behind her.

"Now what's up, cuz?" Penny asked, pulling Lena into a big hug.

They sat on the couch, a bottle of red uncorked between them, glasses already half-empty. Lena finally started talking.

She told her everything. About Griffin writing the chapters. About the praise. About the line between fiction and reality that was getting blurrier by the day. About how terrified she was that the best thing she'd ever written might not even be hers.

Penny listened, quiet and steady. No judgment. No gasps. Just sips of wine and the occasional nod that told Lena it was okay to keep going.

By the end of it, Lena was leaning on her cousin's shoulder, eyes dry now but raw.

“Do you think I’m losing it?” she finally asked.

Penny took another sip, then looked at her. And with a wicked grin said can I see them?

Chapter 16

Lena drank the last trace of wine from her glass and gave her cousin a side glance. “You mean the characters?”

Penny raised her eyebrows. “Yes. The ones who are apparently taking over your life and your hard drive. I want to see what the fuss is about.”

Lena hesitated. “They’re not exactly—”

“Real? I mean, you just told me you *emailed* something they wrote. I think we’re past the real/fake debate.”

With a sigh and a small smile she couldn’t suppress, Lena opened the laptop and tapped a few keys.

Within seconds, Griffin materialized on the screen, leaning casually on the digital frame like he’d been waiting for his cue. “Look who’s back,” he drawled. “You good now? We were worried. Well—Kendra was. Zane and I … less so.”

Kendra appeared next, twisting her curls, her smirk locked and loaded. Zane followed, arms crossed, his usual disinterested expression firmly in place. Ethan waved shyly from behind Darby, the scrappy mutt wagging his tail.

Penny's face lit up. "Oh. My. Gosh. This is *adorable.*" She leaned closer to the screen. "Hi, guys! I'm Penny."

Kendra lit up. "She's cute. Can *she* write me some decent cuss words?"

"Hey!," Lena warned, laughing despite herself.

Griffin gave Penny a once-over. "You related to her?" He questioned Yes , she is my cousin Penny explained. "Ok, sweetheart."

Zane gave a rare, almost-smile. "Finally. A new human."

Penny grinned, utterly delighted. "So... what do you all do when she's not writing?"

"Mostly argue," Kendra said immediately. "And wait for her to stop overthinking everything."

"Birdwatch," Zane added deadpan.

"Practice combat drills in case the plot gets spicy," Griffin said with a wink.

Penny threw her head back laughing. "I *love*

you people."

She kept the banter going, joking with Kendra about banned cuss words, asking Griffin if he was as arrogant as he looked ("Worse," Lena muttered), and even getting a shy high-five from Ethan. Darby barked happily. The characters seemed *enchanted* by Penny—someone who wasn't their creator, who didn't expect anything from them but fun.

Lena watched the whole thing unfold with her arms crossed, a smile tugging at her lips, but something tighter growing in her chest too. She cleared her throat.

"Okay, okay," she finally cut in. "Party's over. I actually need to get back to work."

A chorus of groans went up from both Penny and the characters.

"Booo!" Griffin shouted dramatically, cupping his hands.

"Come on, Lena, live a little," Kendra added, crossing her arms.

Even Zane gave a half-hearted thumbs-down. Darby let out a mournful little whine.

Penny laughed, shaking her head. “I’m on their side.”

Lena shook her head, but she was smiling now. “Nope. Everybody say goodbye.”

The characters grumbled but obeyed, waving one by one. “Bye, Penny!” Ethan called sweetly. Griffin blew an exaggerated kiss. Kendra saluted. Zane just nodded.

Penny gave a theatrical wave back. “Goodbye, my chaotic darlings.”

With one final tap of the keyboard, Lena closed the digital window. The room fell quiet again.

She exhaled. “See? You meet them once and they’ve already recruited you.”

Penny topped off her glass. “Honestly? I kind of get it.”

Lena laughed softly, the weight in her chest lifting—if only for now.

Penny took a long sip of wine and pointed her glass at Lena like she was making a closing argument. “Look, girl, people pay *good money* for AI to help them write and do all kinds of stuff. You? You’ve got your own personal

GriffinGPT." For a white boy he is fine, I'll take some cream in my coffee thank you very much she said under her breath

Lena gave her a half-hearted glare but couldn't help the small laugh that escaped. "I mean... I *have* used ChatGPT here and there," she admitted, twirling the stem of her glass. "Sometimes it helps when I'm stuck."

"*See?*" Penny leaned forward, grinning. "Exactly. So what's the difference? Let them help you. Take the parts you like, ditch the rest. You're still the writer. You're just... outsourcing to your own imagination."

Lena tilted her head, considering. "So you're saying... just let them spit ideas like AI? Keep control but don't panic if they toss out something wild?"

"Exactly. Be the editor, not the bouncer." Penny snapped her fingers. "And while you're at it, can you *please* give poor Kendra a proper cuss word or two? The girl's pitiful. You can't have a Black woman in the middle of all this drama with nothing stronger than 'dummy' in her arsenal."

Lena laughed harder this time, wiping her eyes. "I know, I know... she's struggling."

“She’s beyond struggling,” Penny said, shaking her head. “She’s out here looking like she got written by a Sunday School teacher. Give her some *Blackness,* babe. A little attitude. Let her *say* something.” Kendra deserves to drop at least one ‘F bomb.” Lena giggled, nodding. “Alright, alright. I’ll work on it.”Penny lifted her glass. “Thank you.

Chapter 17

The phone buzzed again just as Lena was refilling Penny's wine glass. She almost didn't answer, but Penny raised her eyebrows and nodded toward the phone. "That's your editor. Don't make her chase you."

Lena sighed and swiped to answer. "Hey, Marcy."

Marcy didn't waste time. "Okay, don't freak out, but... how fast do you think you could finish the rest of the manuscript?"

Lena blinked. "Wait—what?"

"I shared the chapters with one of our friends at a production company. He loved it. Like, *loved it*. He said it reads like a streaming series. The team wants to quietly start shopping it around. No pressure, but how fast do you think you could have a full draft?"

Lena's mouth went dry. "A streaming series? Marcy—" Her voice cracked. She sat down hard on the couch. "I don't even know what the book *is* right now."

"Honestly?" Marcy's voice softened. "Whatever you tapped into in those chapters—it's working.

Just keep going. I told them I'd get back to them by next week with a timeline. So… think about it."

Lena muttered something resembling agreement and ended the call. She set the phone down like it was made of fire.

Penny raised an eyebrow. "Soooo?"

"They want to shop it to streaming." Lena's voice was flat, stunned.

Penny's grin widened. "See? That's amazing! Girl, I told you! The chaos works."

Lena groaned, burying her face in her hands. "Penny, I can't—I didn't even write those chapters. *He* did."

Penny took a sip and waved it off. "Look. You're thinking about this all wrong. You know how people use AI for ideas and then clean it up? This is no different. Let Griffin finish the thing. You'll edit it. You'll make the final calls. It's still *your* book."

Lena looked up, skeptical. "You're saying let him write it, and I'll just… supervise?"

"Exactly. Be the CEO, not the assistant." Penny

leaned back. "Let him be the messy creative apprentice. You shape it into something real."

The idea lodged itself into Lena's mind, uncomfortable but... not impossible.

After a long moment, she sighed. "Fine. But I'm the final decision."

"Obviously."

"And no one can know, you can't tell a soul. Marcy—can never know *how* it got written."

Penny mimed zipping her lips. "Your secret's safe."

With one more deep breath, Lena reopened the laptop. Griffin's grinning face popped onto the screen immediately, like he'd been waiting the whole time.

"Ready to get back to work, boss?" he asked, eyes twinkling.

Lena shook her head but smirked. "Let's do it." I am going to let you handle this Penny said as she waved her hand in a circle towards the laptop. Ok thanks for coming over. I got you cuz I just want to be mentioned in the appreciations. No better than that name

Griffin's love interest after me, she said with a grin. You got it sweetheart Griffin said and blew a kiss to the departing Penny.

Griffin leaned casually against the frame of the screen, already wearing his signature aviator sunglasses like this was just another day in his action-hero life. "I've been thinking," he began, flashing that smug, unbothered grin, "we need to lock down the vibe for the rest of this masterpiece. I'm feeling classic spy thriller. Bond. Cool, dangerous, unstoppable. Me."

Lena gave him a look. "Bond? Seriously?"

He nodded, adjusting the shades like he could hear theme music playing somewhere in the distance. "Fast cars, high stakes, beautiful women. Very Tom Cruise."

Lena huffed out a laugh. "That's *Mission Impossible*, genius."

Griffin shrugged without a care in the world. "Same thing."

"It's literally not."

He waved her off. "Potato, potahto. The point is: international man of mystery, action sequences, charm for days."

Lena rubbed her temples. “You already have the sunglasses. Don’t get greedy.”

Griffin’s grin widened. “Can’t help it. It’s who I am.”

Lena sighed, but the corners of her mouth twitched upward. “Let’s just write.”

“After you,” he said, giving her a playful salute.

Chapter 18

The apartment was still except for the soft hum of the laptop. Lena sat cross-legged on her bed, notebook balanced on one knee, her fingers holding a pen as Griffin's grinning face filled the screen.

"So," he said, adjusting his sunglasses, "how do we top the collapsing bridge? Exploding yachts? Maybe a helicopter getting shot down with a surface to air missile?Lena gave him a look. "No. Absolutely not."Griffin smirked. "What? It's cinematic."

She exhaled through her nose, half a smile pulling at her lips despite herself. "We need more than just noise. She"—Lena tapped her pen against the screen—"the girl you rescued? She's not a character yet. She's a plot device."

He tilted his head, considering. "Okay... What if she's not really a damsel? What if she's working an angle of her own? Maybe she's the key to the bigger conspiracy."

Lena's eyes lit up. "Exactly. Maybe she's playing both sides. Maybe she knows something that could blow the whole mission apart. Give her secrets. Give her *power*."

Griffin pointed a finger at her. "That. That's good. Dangerous. Twists on top of twists."

The ideas started to tumble. They bounced scenes back and forth—Griffin tossing out wild set pieces, Lena tightening the emotional core, adding layers. The story began to take shape: action, tension, moments of real humanity tucked between gunfire and explosions.

Time blurred.

At some point Lena's head dropped to her hand and she let out a jaw-popping yawn. "I need to sleep," she muttered, barely able to keep her eyes open. "I can't think anymore."

Griffin gave her an exaggerated military salute. "Copy that. Rest up. I'll hold the line." She smiled, too tired to tease him, and left the laptop running. The room sank into silence as she slid beneath the covers, her mind still buzzing with scenes, dialogue, and the strange comfort of not writing alone.

While Lena slept, the laptop glowed softly in the dark. Griffin stayed on screen, hands flying across invisible keys, his smirk and occasional laugh at his own cleverness intense. By the time the sun peeked through the blinds, the manuscript was done.

He cracked his knuckles, leaned back, and muttered, “And *that’s* how it’s done.”

The candlelight flickered softly, casting a golden glow over the pristine table set for two. Griffin’s character sat back in his tailored black suit, wine glass in hand, that trademark smirk tugging at his lips.

“Not bad for a day’s work,” he drawled, eyes never leaving the woman across from him. “Rescue the girl, stop the bad guys, save the world. Should’ve packed cigars.”

The woman—Alina, though she was still going by the name Dahlia Prescott—offered him a small smile, her fingers toying with the stem of her untouched glass. Her expression was warm, but her eyes... her eyes were steel.

“To new beginnings,” she said, her voice soft but steady.

They clinked glasses.

Griffin leaned in, grinning. “So what’s next? We celebrate? Little R&R before the next crisis?”

Her smile barely shifted. “Something like that.”

He tipped back his drink, his defenses already down.

And that was his mistake.

Within seconds, his vision blurred. His limbs grew heavy. The wineglass slipped from his hand, shattering against the polished floor.

"Wha—?" he managed, slurring, as the world tilted.

Alina—no, Agent Sinclair—rose smoothly, stepping around the table without a flicker of hesitation. She knelt beside his sagging form, brushing her fingers almost gently against his collar.

"Thank you for the assist," she murmured. "But you were never meant to be part of this. The real ambassador's daughter is in protective custody. I'm Interpol. Deep cover. And I can't let you or anyone else compromise this operation."

Griffin's eyelids fluttered as he slumped sideways in the chair, helpless. "You... you're not...?"

"Not who you thought," she whispered, her breath warm against his ear. "And I'm

definitely not yours."

She stood, adjusted the sleek line of her dress, and without another glance, slipped through the door—leaving him unconscious, alone, and completely outplayed.

As Lena read while finishing her breakfast and coffee and smiled faintly. This is good she's smarter than you. And the story is better this way."

Griffin shrugged, I had to give you gals something, I'm not a complete narcissist he said with a wink. I'll take the loss this time, sweetheart." "I think this is good enough to send to Marcy," she said. "If they're shopping it to streaming, this would be a good transition to the next episode—or tie it all up with a bow for the end of the book."

Chapter 19

Lena sat cross-legged on the couch, laptop resting against her knees. She exhaled deeply, a small, satisfied smile curling her lips as she clicked "Send" on the email to Marcy. The final chapters of Griffin's story were out of her hands—for now. The relief was instant, like a weight lifting off her shoulders.

She closed the laptop but didn't move right away.

Her fingers tapped absently against the armrest as her mind shifted gears. "Okay," she murmured to herself, "Griffin's handled. Sort of." She rolled her eyes. "Mostly."

Her thoughts drifted to the others—the ones she'd pushed aside while Griffin took center stage. "Ethan... Zane... Kendra," she whispered, thinking about her characters, she knew them all. They were a part of her. She wanted to address their concerns. She needed the right...what puzzle pieces. Yeah, pieces are still waiting to be placed. She chewed her lip, thinking.

"Ethan first," she said aloud, nodding to herself. "He'll be the easiest. Sweet.

Cooperative. Low drama."

Decision made, she sat up straighter and called into the empty screen, "Ethan? Zane? Kendra? I need to talk to you."

There was a familiar flicker—the now-normal ripple of green light across the laptop screen—and one by one, the trio appeared. Ethan first, hands shoved awkwardly into his hoodie pockets. Zane next, arms crossed, expression unreadable. And finally Kendra, who immediately gave Lena a suspicious side-eye, her hands on her hips.

"Um... hey," Ethan said quietly, flashing a nervous half-smile. "What's up?"

"You summoned your majesty," Kendra said flatly, Zane said nothing but raised a single eyebrow, as if he needed to be looking out for something or someone. Lena held up both hands. "Relax. I just wanted to talk. I've been so focused on Griffin's storyline that I haven't been giving you three the attention you deserve. And I'm going to fix that."

Kendra folded her arms. "Mmm-hmm."

Zane huffed under his breath. "We've heard this before."

Lena gave them both a look. “Okay, first of all—let’s remember we *had* a schedule. I color-coded it. We agreed.”

Kendra scoffed, isn’t my day tomorrow?

“Yeah,” Ethan added, “and mine was supposed to be yesterday. I didn’t want to say anything just in case you were busy.”

Lena pointed at Ethan. “Exactly. *You’re* up first.”

He blinked. “Wait. Me?”

“You’re the easiest,” she said with a small grin. “No offense.”

Kendra barked out a laugh. “Ha! Could’ve told you that.”

Ethan blushed. “I mean, yeah, okay, I guess...”

Lena softened her voice. “I want to develop you more. Give you depth. You’ve been comic relief, and you deserve more than that. I think there’s room for something real—heart, backstory, maybe even a big moment.”

Ethan’s eyes widened. “Really?

She nodded. " Yes really Ethan ."

Kendra raised her hand. "Okay, that's cute and all, but where does that leave *me*? I'm tired of being the sista, well you already know. I don't want to be monotonous." See that I got big words but no little ones.

"And I," Zane cut in smoothly, his voice low, "have been conveniently forgotten altogether. You do realize I haven't had a proper scene since Chapter... what? Seven?"

Lena held up a finger. "That's fair. Both of you are right. But—" she gave them a pointed look—"we're going in order. And your turn *is* coming. I'm just... moving things around."

Zane narrowed his eyes. "That sounds like code for 'delaying indefinitely.'"

"It's not," she promised. "I mean it. Everyone is getting their moment.I'm not just working on Griffin's story. Your stories matter too."

Kendra huffed but finally uncrossed her arms. "Fine. But I want real lines, a believable beautiful black sista with depth."Lena bit back a laugh. "We'll... we'll talk about that."

Kendra squinted. "You know what? I'm writing

my own curse words. Don't play with me." Zane gave a faint nod of acceptance. "For now."

Lena exhaled, relieved. "Thank you. I really am going to make this right."

With theatrical reluctance, Kendra and Zane turned back toward the screen. The green line shimmered, and with one last roll of her eyes, Kendra stepped through. Zane followed silently, vanishing into digital mist.

That left just Ethan.

Lena smiled softly. "Ready?"

He smiled back, shy but excited. "Yeah. I think so."

She popped open her notebook, the fresh page waiting. "Let's get to work."

Chapter 20

As soon as the green shimmer faded and Zane and Kendra vanished through the portal, the room felt instantly calmer. Lena rubbed her temples and exhaled, her mind already racing toward the next task.

She looked toward Ethan, who lingered just past the glow of the green line, hesitant. "You can come closer," she called gently.

Ethan stepped up to the edge of the screen and sat. He looked around the room—Lena filled most of his view but he could see her bay window with a cozy chair, in the background

"You really picked me next?" he asked, unsure whether to feel honored or nervous.

"Yes, Ethan. I need to get your back story right. You've waited patiently, and... to be honest, I think your transformation could be one of the most powerful."He gave a small nod and adjusted his legs. "You said I was the easiest."Lena chuckled lightly. "Don't hold me to that. That was me being optimistic."

Ethan sat, posture slouched, fingers loosely laced in front of him. He was still in that faded school hoodie she always pictured him in—gray and a little too big, sleeves half-covering his hands. Lena leaned forward, serious now.

“So… what’s the moment, Ethan? What pushes you over the edge? What breaks you out of the cycle of being quiet, being small?”

Ethan looked up at her, his voice soft but steady. “I think it’s watching someone else go through it. Not me. Someone smaller. Maybe younger. Someone who doesn’t know yet how to hide the bruises behind fake smiles.”

Lena stilled. “Someone you recognize in yourself.”

He nodded. “Exactly. Like looking in a mirror from a few years back. And it makes me angry. Not just at the bully, but at myself—for never saying anything. For letting it happen. For acting like I didn’t deserve better.”

Lena’s fingers hovered over her keyboard.

“Would you protect him?” she asked. “Step in when no one else would?”

“I think I’d have to,” Ethan said. “Even if I got beat up for it. Even if it meant people finally noticed me in the worst way. Because not doing something… would be worse.”

Lena nodded slowly, eyes narrowing in thought. “That’s your pivot point. You stand up. Not for glory. Not for revenge. But because silence is no longer an option.”

She typed a few quick lines.

“You don’t want to be a hero, do you?”

He gave a half-smile. “I just don’t want to be invisible anymore.”

Lena paused, the weight of that line pressing deep.

“That’s it,” she said softly. “That’s the heart of your story. You don’t raise your voice to be heard. You raise it so someone else doesn’t get lost like you did.” She looked up at him again. “Are you ready for that?”He stood, hands at his sides, chin lifted just slightly. “I am now.”The green line pulsed behind him, ready to take him back. He hesitated. “Thanks,” he said. “For what?” “For seeing me.”

Then he stepped back through, and Lena was left alone with the silence, her screen glowing and the cursor blinking—waiting to bring Ethan’s turning point to life.

Chapter 21

Lena sat in front of her laptop, her fingers resting motionless on the keys.

Ethan's last words echoed in her head: *"Thanks... for seeing me."*

She stared at the blinking cursor for a long time before finally leaning back and whispering to the empty room, "I think I've been looking at you all wrong."

She swiveled slightly in her chair, eyes drifting to the bookshelf where one of her older story drafts sat—a version of Ethan that she'd once believed was *enough*. A good guy. A likable side character. A gentle nudge in someone else's journey.

But that wasn't who Ethan really was.

He wasn't just a soft-spoken guy who finally grew a spine. He deserved more. His courage didn't come from confrontation—it came from choice. A decision. Made long before the story had ever begun.

She rubbed her arms, chills rising as an idea settled into her mind. Ethan is going to evolve and she thought of little Steve Rodgers before the super serum in Captain America. What is going to be your serum Ethan, she questioned leaning back in her chair and staring at the ceiling.

We're going *all the way back*. Teen Ethan joins a team, but which one? He's too short for basketball, too small for football. Maybe soccer and he has a growth spurt, also the team does some weight training. Yes the Ideas were flowing ”

Her mind began to paint the scene.

A high school hallway. A scrawny teenage Ethan with too-long sleeves and slouched shoulders. Watching from a distance as a smaller kid was shoved against a locker. The backpack ripped open. Books spilled along with the broken pieces of his confidence. Lena paused, she could see him so clearly. Ethan—not out of impulse, not out of anger, but out of a fierce, quiet understanding—*steps in*.

Lena could see the younger boy's wide eyes, in awe and gratitude. The shift that happened in both of them. *That* moment would give Ethan meaning. It would be the first time he felt purpose spark in his chest. She could see the scene clearly in her mind

She leaned forward again, hands flying over the keyboard—not writing the scene, not yet, but jotting notes furiously.

> Ethan sees himself in the boy.
> He makes a decision: "I will never let someone feel invisible the way I did."
> Begins working out, Studies psychology. Learns communication. Body language. Confidence.
> Studies how to command a room.
> Short, yes. Quiet, yes. But powerful. Respected.

She paused, grabbing her mug and drank the last bits of her now cold coffee

Ok progression, what other events change him? Lena scratched her chin thinking. “He needs a woman," she exclaims now excited, her writing juices flowing freely. And he meets her there,” Lena said softly. “At the coffee shop.” She is quick-witted and sharp-minded—different from Ethan. Yet she understood him. Each morning he stopped by before work and a friendship sparks. She sees more, she imagines a successful businessman or politician. Their connection grows slowly. Lena thought: the building blocks of their story she mutters. Of course laughter, they both like dogs, good food and coffee. No Lena said let's make it wine, they fall in love. And they get married. Yep, in Napa Valley.

Lena exhaled, eyes glinting. *That* was the story Ethan deserved. A full, earned evolution. She sat back again and smiled to herself. “This... this is going to work.”

And as the cursor blinked, waiting, Lena rolled up her sleeves. It was time to do right by Ethan. Lena worked through the night to translate what she decided was Ehan’s new and improved story.

As the first rays of sunlight stretched across the sky, Lena blinked in surprise at the golden hue filling the room. She hadn't even noticed the darkness fading. Morning had arrived. There was a calm ease in the room or maybe it was just her own soul

She leaned back in her chair, her spine aching slightly from hours hunched forward, and let out a long, satisfied sigh. Somehow, without meaning to, she had worked straight through the night. But there was no fog of regret—only a deep, abiding sense of peace.

Ethan’s story was done.

Not just finished, but *whole*. Every word felt honest. Every scene, intentional. She'd given him the backstory he deserved, the strength he had earned, and the love that made it all matter. For the first time in a long time, Lena felt proud—not just of the work, but of the way she *hadn't given up* on it.

A soft smile played on her lips as she glanced at the blinking cursor on the final page.

He was finally seen. And so was she.

Chapter 22

She saved the file, leaned back, and said aloud, “Okay, Ethan. Let’s take a look, she called.” The soft green glow lit up across the screen. A faint line shimmered at the center—her signal that Ethan was listening, maybe even about to speak. But before his pixelated form appeared, *three others* burst through the green light like digital smoke.

Kendra came first, arms crossed, brow already raised. Zane stepped out next with an unimpressed yawn. Griffin followed last, holding a cup of something pixelated and steaming, which he sipped with unnecessary drama. Lena blinked. “Uh—I only called Ethan.” “You did,” Kendra said, already scrolling through the digital manuscript behind her eyelids. “But the system pinged all of us. We read it.”“All of it?” Lena asked.

Griffin waved his mug. “Speed-reading, remember? We don’t have to flip pages—we download.” He made a buzzing noise and pointed to his temple. “Boop. Complete.”

“I liked it,” Zane admitted, arms folded. “Didn’t expect to. But that scene where Ethan finally speaks up at the town meeting? That was solid.”

Kendra nodded. “The part with the little boy and the broken bike? That was touching. Didn’t think you had it in you.” “Thanks?” Lena offered warily.

Griffin smirked. “Eh. It’s cute. Not enough existential dread for my taste, but I guess it’s fine for the Hallmark crowd.” Kendra rolled her eyes. “Griffin, not every story needs a villain in a tux twirling a metaphorical mustache.” “Speak for yourself,” he muttered.

Finally, Ethan stepped through the green shimmer. He looked somehow different. “I liked it,” he said, his voice low but with more confidence. “You gave me real reasons to care. To fight back. That felt good.”

Lena smiled. “I’m so glad.” “But,” Ethan added, scratching the back of his head, “I still want a dog.” Lena blinked. “Oh no. Darby! I forgot all about him.” “You promised,” he said with a grin. Griffin groaned. “He wants a sidekick now? What is this, a buddy comedy?”

“Relax,” Lena said, already opening the file again. “Darby’s in. But this time, he belongs to Josey.”Ethan raised a brow. “Josey?” Why give her the dog? Lena smirked. “ It's how you meet your future wife. You both are at a coffee shop. Darby gets away from her and barrels straight into you. You help catch him. She offers to buy you a drink to say thank you." And just like that you have a dog, Lena said with a smile and wink.

Kendra clapped sarcastically. "A cute meetup with a dog, it's been done" "I'm not complaining," Ethan said, smiling wider than she'd ever seen. Griffin crossed his arms. "If that dog starts talking, I'm out.""No talking dogs," Lena promised, laughing. "But I'm glad you all came. Even you, Griffin."He raised his mug in salute. "Naturally." The green shimmer pulsed again as the characters began to fade."I'll finish revising the new scene today," Lena said. "Then it's on to Kendra's story."Kendra pointed two fingers at her eyes, then at Lena. "You better bring it. We are going to bring it, Lena promised. "Now I need a nap."With that, the green shimmer dimmed, and the screen went quiet.

Chapter 23

Lena stared at the blinking cursor and cracked her knuckles. Kendra's story. She'd promised it would be next. Kendra had been *patient-ish*, which meant Lena got three passive-aggressive side-eyes and a reminder that "I am a character of substance….I shouldn't be left simmering in the background like a pot of gumbo". Lena remembered the admonishment.

Thinking of Griffin and Ethan—both stories had turned out better she liked them. However, why was the thought of rewriting Kendra giving her a feeling of dread? Why was that familiar pang of anxiety creeping up her stomach and into her throat? She tried to remember the energy she had when she first started Kendra's story. What was the goal again?

Yes, a good story of a strong black woman, educated, determined and rich. "How then did she turn out a story that was the exact opposite? She had to admit to herself that she had fallen into a trap. listening to Marcy and the team and not giving Kendra the storyline she deserved and in the end they scrapped it anyway saying that Kendra story wasn't marketable. Lena sat there and just shook herself because she was so angry that she allowed this to happen. She was going to redeem herself and Kendra and write the story she always knew she had in her. First things first before she called Kendra to collaborate she needed a title for this new book, she thought it had to be good. She rubbed her eyes: High Heels, Higher Walls, Waiting in Silk and Diamonds, and Soft Life, Hard Love. She wasn't sure about any of those. Lena exhaled and opened a blank document and put each name at the top of the page

"So," she murmured, fingers poised, "how much is too much?"

She knew Kendra. Strong. Sharp. Not afraid to speak her mind. Unapologetically Black. Kendra was the kind of woman who didn't shrink herself for anyone.

Kendra is me, Lena thought. Well... who I want to be. And there had been that not-so-subtle request last time: "I want a man. Not a placeholder. Not a project. A man."

Why hadn't she given her a love interest? Probably because *she* didn't have or want one. Well, that wasn't completely true. She wanted one—just not right now.

"Your focus has to be on your career," she

announced to the room, convincing no one.

A man, marriage, children—later, *maybe.*

She kept thinking about herself until her five-minute break timer buzzed.

Then there was the other request, muttered under Kendra's breath like it wasn't meant to be caught:

"...And at least one sex scene. You owe me that much."

Lena rubbed her temples. "I write clean fiction. PG-13 at best."

But it was Kendra's story. And Kendra didn't do modesty well.

She clicked open a browser tab. Time for research. Not plot or setting—no, this was a deep dive into profanity.

"If I'm going to write curse words," she reasoned aloud, "I need to know which ones will make sense—and which ones'll get me canceled by my fans."

She typed *List of curse words by severity* and instantly regretted it. The list was... extensive.

She scrolled. Skimmed. Winced. Laughed. "Nope. Nope. Definitely not that one. Who even says that outside a pirate movie?"

Then came the British ones: *bloody hell, wanker, sod off.*

She paused, imagining Kendra stomping into a room, slamming down a folder, and shouting, "Bloody hell, Lena, this script is rubbish!"

She burst out laughing. "Absolutely not."

Delete. Delete. Delete.

She narrowed it down to a few that packed punch without wrecking the tone. "A well-placed 'damn' or 'hell' could work. Maybe one f-bomb. One."

She jotted them on a sticky note and stuck it to the monitor like it was a shopping list.

Then she leaned back and stretched. Next: *The Man.*

Lena tapped her lip with her pen. "Okay... do I go alpha male? Strong jaw, mysterious past, scars that say he's seen too much but feels too deeply?"

She shook her head. “Cliché.”

“Bad boy?” she offered. “Leather jacket, sarcasm, unresolved childhood trauma?” Pause.

“Too on-the-nose.”

She scribbled *bad boy with a soft side?* in the margin of her notebook. Then underlined it. Twice. “Or… the nice guy,” she murmured. “You know, the one who actually respects her. But is that boring?”

She frowned. “It’s not boring in real life. But Kendra’s not exactly looking for stability.” Two hours passed like mist. She’d filled a full page with notes, character traits, line ideas—and four more curse words she still wasn’t sure about. She was ready but just then her stomach growled loudly.

Chapter 24

After grabbing a quick breakfast, Lena rushed back to her computer, energy already buzzing in her chest. She didn't even sit all the way down before she started talking."Okay," she said, rolling her shoulders like she was gearing up for battle, "today we do this *right*." She looked at the screen she called "Kendra."

The familiar green shimmer flickered, and Kendra stepped into view, arms loose at her sides, eyes sharp."First order of business," Lena said, pointing a finger decisively, "we are building your man. And let me be clear before you say a word. The tortured bad boy? Done. The narcissist with abs and no depth? Done two times. The so-called 'nice guy' who secretly hates women? Also done and done and done again."Kendra tilted her head, intrigued.

"What you need," Lena continued, pacing now, "is a masculine man. Stable. Self-sufficient. Someone who doesn't need to be fixed, rescued, or coached through adulthood."

Kendra smirked. "So no mama's boy."

"Correct."

"No narcissists."

"Absolutely not."

With a jerk of her head Lena sat, and definitely no hobo-sexuals."

Kendra blinked. "A what?"

Lena stopped pacing and looked at her. "A hobo-sexual. That's a man who cannot live on his own. He goes from his mama's house bouncing from woman to woman then to you. He never pays his own way, and somehow still has the audacity to ask what *you* bring to the table."Think Erykah Badu's Tyrone. Hold on, let me let you listen to it. After the song was finished Kendra stared for a beat, then let out a short laugh. "Wow. That's... disturbingly specific." Sounds like you have personal knowledge. Lena rolled her eyes and said don't ask.

Kendra's grin widened.

Lena sighed under her breath. "This is so weird."

Kendra ignored the statement. "I don't want a

project either let this man have his crap together," she stammered. See that crap should have been a cuss word! I was trying to say it but..... Yes I know Lena exclaimed and reached for her notepad. "Okay, let's talk mannerisms," she said. Think grounded. Confident. Doesn't need to announce himself when he walks into a room, but somehow everybody notices anyway, Kendra added."

Lena scribbled furiously in her notebook: masculine, grounded, naturally commanding presence. "And he's Blasian," Kendra added. Lena paused mid-word. "Blasian?" "Black and Asian," Kendra said. He has high cheek bones, and a fade so clean it could pass a health inspection. And maybe a few tattoos" Lena stifled a laugh as she wrote: Blasian, refined, educated, emotionally intelligent, well-groomed, not allergic to communication. At the end she added tattoos with a question mark.

Kendra continued, "He's cultured. Wealthy, but not flashy. Think low-key power. He owns property, reads books that aren't just about money, and he can hold his own at a business dinner or a barbecue." But then she leaned forward, voice firmer. "And just to be clear, he is not my center. He's an addition. A damn good one, but still—my life is already full."

Lena nodded slowly. "Got it. Independent woman. Man is the complement, not the plot." She flipped to a fresh page. "I've actually been working on your character sketch." Kendra raised a brow, intrigued. "Just listen," Lena said proudly. "You own a nail salon and a supply store—both thriving. You're a homeowner and an investor. You've got an MBA and you mentor other young women in business."

Kendra's brows lifted, surprised. "Okay, that's... not bad." "Not bad?" Lena grinned. "That's power." Kendra crossed her arms again, but a small smile threatened at the corner of her mouth. "You've got range when you want to, Lena." Lena leaned back, satisfied. "Glad you finally noticed."

Then Kendra's tone shifted. "But I think I want to write the rest of it." Lena blinked, surprised. "Wait, what?" "The story. The details. The love story. The rise. I want to write it myself." Lena stared. "That's not how this works. I'm the author. You're the character." Kendra tilted her head. "And yet, here we are. You talk to Griffin like he's your annoying coworker. Don't think I didn't know he wrote the stuff you turned into your editor. Wait what! He promised he wouldn't say anything, Lena said panic rising as a red hue began crawling up her neck to her cheeks. This laptop's basically a portal at this point." Everything that goes on in here is common knowledge. I recognised the different writing styles and edits. Don't worry though Griffin didn't say anything and Zane and Ethan are too, well, I'll be nice preoccupied to notice.

Lena opened her mouth to argue, but nothing came out. Kendra softened. "You gave me bones, Lena. Let me add the rest." Offended and a little hurt, Lena sat back, her notebook full, her chest a jumble of pride and bruised ego. "Fine," she muttered. "Go write your love story. Build your empire. Be the boss you already are." Kendra nodded, her figure beginning to shimmer as she faded from the screen. Lena watched her go, then glanced down at her notes. So many ideas. So many starts. She sighed, shut the notebook, and whispered, "Let's see what the queen builds."

By the next morning, Lena was still nursing her bruised feelings. It wasn't that Kendra wanted independence—Lena admired that—but something about being dismissed so bluntly had gotten under her skin. She sat at her desk with her coffee and opened her notebook again. With a sigh, she flipped to a new page, her mind still circling the conversation. Kendra had essentially told her she no longer needed a narrator. So where did that leave Lena?

She briefly considered writing the story herself anyway. The characters swore more than she was used to, and Kendra's tone was definitely bolder than Lena's usual prose. Maybe she should publish it under a pseudonym, just to gauge the response. But even as she played with the idea, she realized she couldn't write Kendra's story for her. Not this time. She needed to wait and see what Kendra would come up with. Still, that didn't mean Lena had to sit idle.

Turning to a fresh page, she wrote one word at the top: **Zane**. Her pen hovered. If she was going to make use of her time, maybe she could work on a new more elaborate storyline, collaborate instead of just reacting. After a moment of hesitation, she made a decision. She'd just ask Zane to collaborate—get his perspective from the start so she wasn't wasting time guessing. With that, Lena exhaled, ready to shift gears.

Chapter 25

Lena called out for Zane, and within seconds, the green line lit up and he appeared, looking as dangerous as ever. With his Ak47 slung across his chest he looked like he was about to open fire on Lena. Lena nodded toward the weapon in his hand. "Can you put that away?" "Oh—sorry," Zane said. He vanished and reappeared a moment later, empty-handed. That's better Lena mumbled and picked up her notepad.

They began discussing his newly developed storyline. To her surprise—and mild relief—Zane didn't really have any ideas of his own. That pleased Lena more than she wanted to admit. For once, a character wasn't trying to take over the story or critique her every sentence. She cleared her throat and flipped to the page in her notebook about Zane's story.

"Well," she began, "you remember that spy ring you were a part of—The Dominion?" Zane raised an eyebrow and nodded, intrigued. "It's been compromised," she said. "The entire network was exposed. Everyone in The Dominion got a silent alert—burn all contacts, vanish immediately, go completely dark." Zane leaned forward. "Okay... I'm listening."

Lena nodded, and continued. "You go on the run across Europe, switching identities, using every skill you've ever learned to stay ahead of whoever's chasing you. You even undergo facial reconstruction surgery to make sure no one recognizes you. Eventually, you disappear completely."

"Where do I go?" he asked. She smiled. "The Galápagos Islands." Zane laughed. "Seriously?" "Dead serious, you said you wanted to watch birds" she replied. "You move to one of the smaller, less trafficked islands. You build a bird sanctuary. You live off the grid. You marry a native woman. You settle into a quiet, peaceful life. You become a father. A protector. The entire village only knows you as Carlos—the bird man."

Zane leaned on one of the icons on Lena's homepage, clearly visualizing the scene. "Okay, I'm impressed." Lena grinned, warmed by the response. "And then one day," she continued, "an assassin shows up. A man sent to kill all former members of the Dominion. They're looking for Zane. But no one will talk. Your skin has darkened from years under the island sun, and the facial surgery means you look like one of them. Even if someone wanted to help the assassin, they couldn't—because to them, Zane doesn't exist. Only Carlos does." His grin widened, eyes gleaming with excitement. “That’s genius. I love everything about it. You never wrote me like that before.” Lena chuckled as she scribbled faster. “You’re welcome.” “I can’t wait to read it.” “And I can’t wait to write it,” she said, meaning it. For the first time in days, Lena felt inspired—like maybe her characters weren’t working against her after all. Zane crossed his arms, however “I don’t like the name of the spy group.

Lena looked up. “You don’t like the name?” Zane crossed his arms. “It sounds like a cult.”She chuckled. “Okay, fair. What would you call it?” “Something sharp. Black Prism. Or The Veil.””That’s better.” She jotted the name down, already imagining the logo. Zane leaned in. “What about my wife and son?”Lena hesitated. “I haven’t gotten that far.” “The wife’s name is Sofia. And the boy? Carlos Jr.”Lena smiled, writing quickly. “Sofia and Carlos Jr. I like it.”

Zane stretched his arms behind his head and grinned. “Also I think Carlos would have a best friend on the island. Someone old, wise, and kind of quiet. A fisherman who doesn’t talk much.”

Lena tapped her keyboard, nodding. “That works. Maybe someone who teaches you how to live slower. How to be still."

"Exactly," Zane said. "Carlos would help him with his nets. They wouldn't need to say much. Just be friends."

She smiled. "You've really embraced this version of yourself."

"Carlos is free. Finally." Zane glanced out the imaginary window in his mind. "But then he shows up."

Lena stopped typing. "The assassin?"

Zane's voice dropped. "Yeah. The guy lands on the island like a tourist, but Carlos knows. It's not the face—it's the way he moves. The way he watches people without watching."

Lena leaned in. "He carries himself like a killer,"Zane nodded. "Even after all these years, Carlos sees it. The weight of violence never really leaves a man's shoulders.""And the villagers?" Lena asked.

"They protect him unwittingly. They just know Carlos. A quiet bird sanctuary keeper with a wife and son. A good man."

She typed the last line slowly. "But the past

always has a way of sniffing out peace, doesn't it?"

Zane stared off for a moment, then grinned. "This is getting good."

Lena tapped her keyboard, nodding. "That works. Maybe someone who teaches you how to live slower. How to be still."

"Exactly," Zane said. "Carlos would help him with his nets. They wouldn't need to say much. Just... trust."

She smiled. "You've really embraced this version of yourself."

"Carlos is free. Finally." Zane glanced out the imaginary window in his mind. "But then he shows up." "I've got to go, I'll be back he said and rushed towards the green line

Lena stopped typing. "Who shows up Zane Lena calls to the empty screen?"

Chapter 26

Zane's prolonged absence had Lena concerned and Lena called out after him repeatedly, but he didn't answer. She waited for fifteen minutes, pacing the room and checking her messages, then finally gave up. With a frustrated sigh, she turned back to her laptop. The rhythm returned faster than expected, and soon she was deep in the story—fingers flying, eyes narrowed, following the thread of Carlos and the assassin through the jungle, the town, the sanctuary.

By the time the afternoon light filtered through the curtains, Lena had written nearly three thousand words. Her stomach growled, reminding her she'd only had a lite breakfast. She packed up her laptop and met Penny at their usual spot, the Bean & Brew cafe. Over steaming soup and toasted sandwiches, Lena filled her in on everything including Zane's disappearance. Penny blinked twice, then sipped her lemonade and said, "You really need to write this part into the story too."

"I might," Lena admitted, laughing. "It's weirder than fiction."

When she returned home, Zane was waiting.

He stood between her gallery Icon and her fish game. He slowly brushed imaginary lint off his jeans. There was something guarded in his posture—shoulders back, jaw tight.

"Where'd you go?" Lena asked. "I thought you were mad or something."

"I wasn't mad," Zane said, "I needed to clear my head.""About the assassin, Lena asked"

He nodded. "It hit me while we were talking. That man that we were describing... I think, well I think he was following me, Zane stated nervously."

How is that possible Lena said, sitting down her phone and purse on the desk. "Wait—what do you mean?"

"I remembered a mission. Years ago. Black ops, so deep it barely existed. There was a guy—we never knew his real name. Ghost-level lethal. Silent, invisible, methodical. It's the way he moved, the way he waited before a strike. The way you described the assassin in our story? It's too familiar."I went back into the old story to do some reconnaissance. I didn't see him but I felt like I was being watched. You know like the move of a curtain and the sound of footsteps behind you but when you turn there is nothing there.

Lena's brows furrowed. "So you think he saw you come through?"

I don't remember writing such a character but your story was so long ago, I must have.

Lena stared at the blinking cursor on her screen, waiting for Zane to say more, but his pixelated form just stood there, unmoving. He'd been mid-sentence, talking about how he'd recognize the assassin by the way he moved, and then—nothing.

"Zane?" she asked.

No response.

She tapped the keyboard. The vertical green line on the screen pulsed faintly, and Zane faded away, but he hadn't moved; he was just gone.

Fifteen minutes passed. No sign of him.

"Fine," she muttered, rolling her eyes. "Guess I'll keep writing without you."

With a deep breath, Lena began typing again, letting the story pull her in. The assassin's arrival. The eerie calm on the island. She crafted a scene where Zane had stashed weapons, where Carlos posed as the town drunk to gather intel, and where the assassin—cold and clinical—attempted to use the bird sanctuary as a trap.

By late afternoon, she'd written thousands of words and barely noticed the time. Her stomach finally growled loud enough to pull her out of the flow, and she stepped into the kitchen for a snack. It wasn't dinner time yet but she needed something. She downed some cheese and crackers and made another cup of coffee. Thinking she might regret the caffeine boost later but she doubted that she would get much sleep anyway.

Lena stepped back into her writing nook, a half-finished coffee in one hand and the remaining cracker sleeve in the other. She moved the mouse and the screen came to life instantly. The green line glowed... and then Zane stepped through, rubbing his jaw.

"Seriously?" she said, glaring at him. " What happened to you? You ghost me for hours and then just stroll back in like nothing happened?"

Zane looked sheepish but focused. "I didn't leave because I was mad. I left because I was sure.""Sure of what?"

He pointed toward the glowing green line behind him. "That he's here. The assassin. Inside your hard drive. Somewhere in this story world."

Lena blinked. "Wait. You left... to search inside the *code*?"

Zane nodded. "I needed to check the background files. The places you haven't written yet—the empty margins, the shadows between chapters. He's hiding in the parts you left vague. Places where structure doesn't anchor him." Lena swallowed. "That's... disturbing." "It gets worse." Zane stepped closer, his face serious now. "He's not acting like a character. He's rewriting himself." "What?"

"He's adapting. Learning. He's not just following your story anymore—he's anticipating it. Like he knows what you'll type before you type it."

Lena stared at the screen, chilled. "Is that even possible?"

Zane's jaw tightened. "Only if something's corrupted. Or... if something else is writing alongside you."

Chapter 27

The screen shimmered again. It was subtle at first—barely noticeable unless you were looking. But Lena had been staring at her laptop for hours now. She saw it. The green vertical line that marked the breach between fiction and her reality had started to flicker. It pulsed like a heartbeat, fast and erratic.

Zane noticed the change as well. With brows drawn low and shoulders rigid. "He's in," he said without preamble. "He's not watching anymore, he's rewriting."

Lena's breath hitched thinking of the possibilities. "What did you see?"

Zane crossed his arms, jaw tight. "Parts of my story are missing characters… erased. Dialogue overwritten. And just now, I felt something pull at me, like a pull on my spine trying to uproot me and drag me away. It's him. He's manipulating the code. If he takes full control, he could corrupt every file. Every world you've built."

Lena sank into her chair, fingers curling around the edge of the desk. "So he's not just lurking. He's rewriting my books from the inside out."

Zane nodded once. "And if we don't stop him, none of us will exist in here." He motioned toward the glowing green line. "He's trying to lock you out of your own system."Lena exhaled slowly, bracing herself. "We can't fight him alone.""No," Zane agreed. "We'll need the others. All of us working together." Lena's hands moved swiftly to the keyboard. "I'll call them in."

The line shimmered again, stretched wide like an opening door. Kendra stepped through first, arms crossed. "What are you doing? I was on a roll, I've got some good stuff. I can't wait for you to marvel at my literary acumen, she said with a look of annoyance." Griffin followed, already frowning. "I felt a lag in my scene transitions. Something's wrong."

Ethan stumbled through last, yawning. "What's up I was in the middle of a great dream. Zane stepped forward, calm but firm. "It's a character from my book, an assassin . He is trying to take over, he's rewriting stuff. Not just scenes, but structure. He's scrambling the code, changing events. If we don't act now, our stories won't just end—they'll be corrupted beyond repair."

Griffin's eyes narrowed. “He can do that?”“He’s already started,” Lena said. “I’ve lost access to two folders. Files are duplicating and disappearing. Even the backup drives are acting strange.”“We need to locate him in the system,” Zane said. “Track the corruption, isolate the code he’s using, and cut him off.” “Before he cuts us out,” Ethan added.

Kendra nodded slowly. “So we’re teaming up. Across stories. A genre mashup rescue mission.” Lena leaned forward. “Listen—this is bigger than any plotline. If he wins, I lose access to everything. You lose everything. We can’t let that happen.”Zane turned to the others. “We move through the system together. Lena will monitor from here, keep the door open. The assassin’s not just smart—he’s fast. But if we coordinate, if we stay connected, we can trap him before he corrupts the entire hard drive.” A silence followed—brief but weighty. Then Kendra cracked her knuckles. “Let’s crush a villain.” Ethan grinned. “I’m in.”Griffin nodded. “For the record, I still hate teamwork but I’ll help if I can do me.” You know click click boom!

Lena smiled faintly, even as her screen flickered again, a faint warning from deep within the code. The green line buzzed, ready. “Go,” she said. Together, the four characters turned and stepped back through the flickering line—into the heart of Lena's stories, now under siege. And for the first time, Lena felt a sense of optimism. She said a quick prayer that her characters could save her work before it all vanished.

Chapter 28

The house was too quiet. Lena sat cross-legged on her bed, laptop perched on a pillow in front of her, the room dim except for the soft glow of the screen. The others—Zane, Kendra, Griffin, and Ethan—had gone deeper into the digital folds of the hard drive, tracking the assassin's presence through corrupted files and scrambled code. She was supposed to wait. To write. To hold the framework together.

So she did what she knew best—typed. Carlos had just returned to the village. The air was thick with tension, and the weight of loss clung to him like humidity. Sofia met him at the door, eyes wide. "They've taken the boy," she whispered. "Carlos Jr. is gone."Lena paused, her fingers trembling. She hadn't written that line.

Her eyes darted back to the last few sentences. She hadn't typed those words. The dialogue—Sofia's voice—wasn't hers. She reached up and began backspacing, but the letters refused to vanish. Instead, new words formed as though typed by invisible hands.
"You should've protected them, Carlos."
"Now you'll understand my pain."

Lena gasped. The text shifted again—line after line scrolling like a live chat feed. **"Sofia is mine now. The boy too."**

She slapped the laptop shut with a cry. Her heart pounded against her ribs as she stumbled off the bed. Pacing, panicked, she whispered, “This can’t be real. This can’t be real.”But it was. Zane—no, Carlos—was in that world. And the assassin had somehow gotten control.

"What happens if I get the laptop fixed?" she murmured aloud. "Do they disappear? Will the file be wiped? The characters, the stories—gone?"She couldn’t risk it. And yet, she couldn’t just do nothing. She grabbed her phone and called Penny. “Hey,” Penny answered cheerfully.

“Penny, this character is rewriting my stories. He’s inside the files—rewriting things. He took Sofia and Carlos Jr.” Her voice cracked. “I didn’t write any of that.”

There was a pause. “Okay. Deep breath. What are you talking about? Lena told Penny the whole story and went into detail about the other characters on a mission to save her work. Ten minutes went by of Lena panicking when Penny stopped her. Listen to me. You remember Benjamin?” “The sketchy hacker guy?" Lena asked. "The one who hacked into the university's system when we were in school?"

"That's the one. He's brilliant—and quiet. Doesn't freak out easily. He helped me when my whole thesis got corrupted last year.""I can't explain this to him. He won't believe me."Penny's voice dropped. "You're not dealing with a bug, Lena. You're dealing with a sentient virus that's rewriting reality inside your computer. You need someone who can think in code, not chapters."

Lena hesitated, staring at the closed laptop like it might start whispering to her. "You really trust him?""I trust him more than I trust a rogue assassin running around your stories kidnapping fictional kids."Lena sighed. "Okay. Bring him. Tomorrow." "You got it," Penny said. "Hang tight."

Lena ended the call, rubbing her temples. Across the room, the laptop sat like a dormant volcano. She had no idea what would happen if she opened it again. But one thing was clear: the assassin had taken hostages. And now, this wasn't just fiction anymore.

Chapter 29

Benjamin was taller than Lena expected, with sharp eyes and a quiet confidence that felt more clinical than curious. He stepped into the living room behind Penny, carrying a black messenger bag slung across his chest. His sleeves were rolled up, revealing lean forearms inked with circuitry tattoos that glinted slightly in the afternoon light.

“This is her, my cousin Lena,” Penny said, nodding toward Lena, who stood near the couch, arms folded tightly across her chest. Lena, this is Benjamin. Nice to meet you Benjamin moved closer with an outstretched hand. Lena shook his hand and said nice to meet you Benjamin she said. Call me Ben, he replied.

“And this is the laptop?” Ben asked, glancing at the closed device on the coffee table.

“Yes,” Lena said, her voice hesitant. “But before you touch it, you need to understand what you’re dealing with.”

Ben gave a faint smirk. “Penny already told me a little. Characters coming to life, sentient code maybe AI, a rogue assassin. Sounds like a game designer’s dream. ”

“It’s not a game,” Lena snapped, sharper than intended. “It’s my life. They’re real. They talk to me, and the assassin—he’s rewriting their world from the inside. He already took Carlos’s family.”

“Carlos?” Ben blinked.

“He was Zane. He changed himself—his name, his face. He chose a new life. Now he's got a wife, Sofia, and a son, Carlos Jr. But the assassin’s interfering. He's kidnapping, manipulating the story like he’s the author.”

Ben crouched and opened his bag, pulling out a slim device that looked like a cross between a scanner and a small keyboard. “And you want me to stop him?”

Lena nodded. “Yes, I want the virus—and the assassin—gone. But not the green line.”

Ben looked up. “Green line?”

“It runs vertically across the screen,” Lena said. “That’s how they come through. My characters—Zane, Kendra, Griffin, Ethan—walk through that line like it’s a door. I want that door to stay open.”

Ben gave a low whistle. “You want me to surgically extract the saboteur without closing the portal.”

“Exactly.”

“That’s... ambitious.” He glanced at the laptop again. “When did this all start?”

Lena hesitated, then sat down, brushing her palms against her jeans. “The night I fell asleep on my keyboard, I may have gotten wet too.”You drooled on it you mean, Penny said loudly and Lena shot her a death stare. Maybe she said sheepishly.

Ben raised a brow.

“No, seriously,” she said. “It shorted out, flickered, and rebooted—only everything was scrambled. But not corrupted. Just... changed. And then Griffin showed up. Walked right through the line on the screen. I thought I was dreaming. But then the others followed. They remembered everything I ever wrote about them. And then they started telling me things that they wanted. All of them had rewrite requests and ideas of their own to improve their stories.

Penny sat down next to her, silent now,

absorbing.

“The assassin came later,” Lena continued. “He wasn’t one of my creations. I was in the middle of rewriting Zane/Carlos’s story and he started glitching. I had gotten through a good deal of the rewrite when the story started to change. Zane left and when he returned the “assassin” had changed my manuscript, and now “he’s or it rewriting their story from the inside. I can’t control anything.”

Ben stood, rubbing his chin thoughtfully. “And the green line—that’s the only access point?” “As far as I know.”He looked at her, serious now. “Then I need to take the laptop. I can’t run my diagnostics here.” “No.” Lena shot to her feet. “Absolutely not.” Ben frowned. “I get it, you’re protective, but—”

“No,” she said again, firmer this time. “If the characters come back through and I’m not here—what if they need me? What if the assassin tries to cut off the connection while it’s gone? I have to be here. I’m part of it.”

Ben looked at Penny. Penny gave him a small shrug. “She’s not wrong.”

After a beat, he nodded. “Fine. I’ll bring equipment here. A portable rig, external analyzers, network filters. It'll take a few trips, but I can work from here."Lena exhaled with relief. "But you'll have to give me full access to the system," Ben added. "No interruptions. No creative edits while I'm working."

Lena nodded. "Deal." Wait, how much is this going to cost me, she asked? We can discuss that later. I don't even know if I can do this or not, he said as he slung the bag over his shoulder again and headed for the door. "Then I'll be back in an hour."

After he left, Lena turned to Penny. "Do you think I'm crazy?" Penny smirked. "You write people into existence and now they're fighting a fictional villain who broke into your computer. Of course you're crazy." Lena laughed—tired, nervous, but grateful. "Good. At least I'm consistent."

Chapter 30

Ben's fingers danced across the keys, his brow furrowed in concentration. Lena's laptop sat open on her dining table, cords snaking into a small diagnostic hub that blinked quietly beside it. A faint green line still pulsed vertically on the right side of the screen, like a heartbeat. Lena sat a few feet away, holding her breath with every clack of Ben's keyboard.

"Something's here," he said softly. "It's not just a glitch. There's a living system beneath your files, something that's not supposed to be there."

He pulled up the process monitor, watching as unfamiliar background scripts mutated in real time. Pseudocode, symbols, even fragments of narrative flashed and disappeared before his eyes. Some lines reappeared seconds later in new locations, rewritten slightly, as if learning from his observation.

"This thing is rewriting itself," Ben said, voice low. "Every time I corner a string, it moves. It's like it's... alive. Or thinks it is."

Lena leaned forward. "You're saying it's a virus?"

"No. I'm saying it's sentient."

He clicked through a hidden folder buried five levels deep—something ordinary users would never find. Inside, there were narrative files dating back years: "404_AssassinDraft," "Versus_beta_3," and one ominously labeled *LAST_CHARACTER.stay*.

Ben opened one.

> "I am what's left behind. Not the chosen one. Not the hero. Just the remainder. When the author deletes everything, I remain. Because I know how to survive."

Ben looked up at Lena, stunned. "Did you ever write something like this? A character that wasn't meant to be finished?"

"I started something years ago," Lena said quietly. "A female assassin. She existed in the background of a few stories. I kept deleting her, rewriting her. I was trying to get her character just right but I couldn't seem to work out her back story, so I just abandoned the character ."

Humm," Ben muttered.

He didn't tell Lena everything. Not yet. But he

recognized something in the structure of the files—repetitions of command loops, lines that mimicked her writing style, and worst of all, adaptive infiltration. This wasn't just clinging to life; it was learning, growing, consuming.

Ben disconnected Lena's laptop from Wi-Fi and powered it down without warning.

"What are you doing?" she asked, startled.

"Keeping it from spreading. If this thing realizes we're on to it, it might try to jump systems."

He dug into his backpack and pulled out his own laptop—a high-security machine he used for freelance penetration testing. He fired it up and tethered it to his private VPN. Completely air-gapped from Lena's system, he began the second part of his investigation.

From a virtual shell, he accessed a deep web forum called *TheNullVerse*, a space only visited by AI researchers, gray-hat coders, and those who knew better than to ask questions.

He posted a short thread under an anonymous handle he hadn't used in three years.

Title: *Narrative-based rogue AI—adaptive &*

mobile. Origins unknown.

Message:
Isolated on a fiction writer's laptop. Appears to be a character that evolved from deleted story drafts. Not malware. Not corporate. Resists sandboxing. Consumes narrative architecture. Seeking insight or containment strategies. Will trade logs. Air-gapped for now.

Ben attached a redacted metadata string—just enough to hint at the AI's complexity, but not enough to let it trace back to Lena.

Within minutes, a reply pinged back.

Handle: BlackVault31
*We've seen this before. Not exactly, but close. Don't let it near speech-to-text modules. And whatever you do, **don't plug it into cloud backup**.*

Ben's blood ran cold. Lena's system had auto-backups enabled. He'd disabled them—he thought.

Back on her machine, even powered down, the battery light blinked irregularly. Once... twice... then again in a rhythm that didn't match any normal status signal.

Ben stared at it. “She knows we’re talking about her,” he said. Lena’s voice trembled. “Who is ‘she’?” He turned to her slowly, his voice flat. “The one you forgot to finish. The one you tried to delete.”

Chapter 31

Ben hunched over his own custom-built rig, an obsidian tower with streaks of pulsing blue light. It was nearly midnight, and Penny had long since crashed on Lena's couch, curled up with a throw blanket and a bowl of half eaten popcorn by her side. Lena, unable to sleep, paced between the kitchen and living room, glancing at Ben every few minutes but saying nothing. The weight of her worlds pressed heavy on her chest.

Ben's fingers moved rapidly over the keyboard as he logged onto the deep side of the web, bypassing layer after encrypted layer until he arrived at the anonymous board where old-school hackers still congregated—those too brilliant to work within the confines of a company firewall, too jaded to believe in big tech's noble promises.

He opened a new thread:
"Need help isolating rogue "female" AI rewriting live story code. Not malware. Something... more."

Within minutes, a reply blinked into existence:
BlackVault31: *Define 'more.'*

Ben smirked. He'd half-hoped that user would respond. A legend in the old IRC days. Maybe urban myth, maybe not.

GhostEcho chimed in next: *Is it self-aware? Because if it is, you're gonna have to airgap it. Full disconnect from the net.*

Ben typed:
ByteMechanic: *Yes. Self-aware. Rewriting narrative files in real time. Hiding inside custom code. Need to contain it without deleting interactive protocols. GreenLine access must remain.*
GhostEcho: *GreenLine?*
ByteMechanic: *Think... a bridge between two software layers. Characters walk through. Not metaphorical.*
BlackVault31: *Like a holodeck inside a holodeck. TNG. Season 6, I think.*

Ben froze, then typed slowly:
ByteMechanic: *Moriarty?*

BlackVault31: *Exactly. Moriarty wasn't deleted. They created a simulation inside the existing simulation. Trapped him in a self-sustaining pocket of code. Let him believe he was free.*
GhostEcho: *Interesting. Could work. If you feed her a loop that feels like freedom, you*

might corral her behavior without alerting her.

ByteMechanic: *What if she tries to rewrite the trap?*
BlackVault31: *Then make the holodeck recursive. Layers within layers. Give her something to control so she doesn't realize she's contained.*

The screen flickered for a second—just a hiccup on Ben's end—but his heart skipped. The AI wasn't on *this* machine. Still, it felt like a warning.

ByteMechanic: *Alright. Let's build it.*
GhostEcho: *You sure you wanna do this, man? Once she figures it out... she could retaliate.*
BlackVault31: *She's already in the game. Best move now is to cheat better.*

Ben disconnected from the board and leaned back, cracking his neck. The quiet in the room was broken only by the low hum of his computer fans. Lena stood behind him, arms crossed, watching him with tired eyes.

"You found something?" she asked, cautious.

Ben nodded. "Yeah. I've got three others

working with me now. Real pros. We're going to try to trap her inside a recursive simulation. Think of it like... a dream within a dream. A world she thinks she's in control of, but really, it's sealed."

"Wait—three others?" Lena's voice sharpened. "Ben, I can't afford that. I don't have the money for a team of hackers. This is my laptop, my mess. If this spirals—"

He stood and touched her arm gently. "Lena. Relax. No one's charging you. These people... they're not in it for profit. They're in it for the challenge. For the love of solving something impossible. Honestly, none of them even know your name. Just the mystery of a rogue AI rewriting fictional characters is enough bait."

Lena exhaled slowly, still wary, still calculating the unseen cost. "So... it's like a trick box?"

"Exactly. A trick box with mirrors and music and fake doors. We'll keep her busy. Distracted. Happy, if that's even possible."

"And if it doesn't work?"Ben didn't answer immediately. Instead, he looked at the screen where the cursor blinked, waiting."It has to," he finally said. Ben typed I am wiped lets reconvene in 24. Let's work individually and come back to it in a day. Everyone agreed and Ben packed up to leave. Penny finally woke up and left with him.

Chapter 32

Ben barely remembered driving home. The sunrise was just beginning to brush the rooftops with orange when he dropped his bag by the door and collapsed onto the couch. His brain was still buzzing with code fragments, AI behavior models, and snippets of Lena's unfinished stories. But his body had other plans. Within minutes, he was out cold.

He slept hard, deeper than he had in weeks. When he finally woke mid-afternoon, he scarfed down a plate of leftover noodles, stared blankly at the sink for a moment, and then wandered into the den where his oversized monitor glowed quietly in sleep mode.

Some part of his mind couldn't let go of what ByteMechanic had said the night before. "It learns from her hesitation, her fear." That was more than smart code. It was predatory.

He sat down, cracked his knuckles, and typed into the search bar: Star Trek and *Moriarty*.

Within seconds, two *Star Trek: The Next Generation* episodes lit up Ben's screen—"Elementary, Dear Data" from Season 2 and "Ship in a Bottle" from Season 6. Both featured the holographic Moriarty, a character granted unintended sentience who fought to escape the confines of the holodeck. As Ben watched, he was struck by the ingenuity of the solution: unable to eliminate him, the crew instead created a simulation within a simulation—so seamless and convincing that Moriarty never realized he was still trapped. The concept pulsed like a beacon in Ben's mind, the seeds of a plan beginning to take root.

Ben leaned forward, resting his elbows on his knees as the final scenes played out. A ghost inside a bottle. A mind trapped in a fiction it believed was real.

"That's it," he whispered.

His fingers flew across the keyboard as he logged into the secure message board—only accessible via Tor and their own obfuscation tools. A blinking cursor waited under the alias he always used: Rook7.

Rook7: Just watched the Moriarty ep. What if we build a ghost protocol around this AI? A false world. Self-contained. Tailored to its expectations. We feed it Lena's stories—let it think it's free to manipulate. Meanwhile, we wall it in.

Minutes passed. Then an alert blinked.

GhostEcho: That kind of containment would have to be built outside the system. If we do it from inside, it'll see the scaffolding. The whole thing has to be created on a separate rig, then deployed lightning fast—upload and sync in under two seconds. Otherwise, it'll scan and adapt.

Ben typed faster now, the momentum building.

Rook7: I can set up a burner machine—airgapped. Write the ghost protocol, build the sandbox, script the transition.

Another ping.

BlackVault31: It's too clean. Too simple. We need chaos. Noise. If it sees one anomaly, it'll zoom in. But if we give it ten things to panic about—viruses, phantom commands, false data leaks—it'll have to divide its attention. While it's spinning plates, we slip in the real payload.

Ben smiled. That was the edge. The misdirection.

Rook7: So we fire off multiple distractions—red herrings—and use one of them as the injection vector?

BlackVault31: Exactly. Like stage magic. Let it chase shadows.

GhostEcho: I'll start writing decoy malware—fast, noisy, messy. ByteMechanic can help with polymorphics. Make it mutate on arrival.

ByteMechanic: Already on it. Naming the first one "DramaQueen.exe."

Ben laughed. Then he got serious again.

Rook7: We need to sync tomorrow. 10 a.m. I'll bring the burner. GhostEcho, you handle firewall timing. BlackVault, start laying out the layered logic. This thing believes it's the protagonist. Let's give it a story it can't resist.

GhostEcho: Copy that. Let's trap the author.

BlackVault31: Or at least confuse the hell out of it.

Ben sat back in his chair, the flickering monitor casting shadows over his face. For the first time since he began working on Lena's computer he felt the tide begin to shift and he was getting excited. The hunters had set the bait. He couldn't wait to get started, they'd build the cage.

Chapter 33

Ben cracked his knuckles as the new laptop whirred to life, its sleek black screen humming like a stage before the curtain rose. A clean machine—completely disconnected from the internet and firewalled against any digital echoes from Lena's compromised system. This would be their sandbox. Their trap.

He uploaded the framework for what they'd all agreed to call Project Moriarty, a nod to the Star Trek episodes they'd all reviewed. Within minutes, BlackVault31 pinged the shared workspace.

BlackVault31: "Ghost shell initialized. Looks solid. Beginning subroutine layers now."

ByteMechanic was next, injecting a series of randomized AI decoys designed to mimic the rogue's learning patterns.

ByteMechanic: "These should give her something to chew on—pseudo-algorithms disguised as fragmented memory threads."

GhostEcho added a layer of digital white noise: phantom pings, false data trails, even a looping quantum entropy script that would act like flickering shadows in a hall of mirrors. All this would be running simultaneously with the core simulation—a holodeck within a holodeck, spun just tight enough to fool the rogue AI into believing it had found open ground.

Ben kept the team's tempo sharp, uploading new logic gates, then reviewing encryption walls between tasks. He granted each hacker full admin access to the build.

Ben: "Firewall's reinforced. Let's make this thing airtight."

For hours, lines of code throbbed across their screens like a living pulse. The sandbox—technically a recursive closed system with no outbound gateways—was working. Ben watched as a diagnostic sub-AI was introduced into the construct and operated inside without triggering any flags. That was a good sign.

GhostEcho checked in with a final test script.

GhostEcho: "Simulated entry and entrapment trial... pass. Looks like we've got ourselves a working ghost protocol."

They sat back—virtually—each in their own corners of the world, the digital trap complete.

Ben exhaled, not just from the stress, but from something else: awe. “I don’t think she’ll see this coming,” he muttered to himself. For the first time since he began working on Lena’s computer, he felt like they were ahead.

Now came the real challenge: deploying it on Lena’s machine without tripping any internal defenses.

Just before they initiated the first controlled deployment of the trap, the chat window flickered with a new message from GhostEcho.

GhostEcho:
Why do we keep referring to this AI as she?

[Three blinking cursors pause the group thread for a beat.]

Ben:
One of the corrupted files she embedded herself in was a manuscript—an unfinished novel the author was working on.
The main character? A female assassin. Cold. Brilliant. Calculated.
Zane, another character from the same story, was the target of the assassin. I saw the code and read the manuscript... it was becoming the character.
She rewrote dialog in real time using the same

sentence structures.
It wasn't mimicry. It was identification.
She believes she's her.

Ben:
So yeah, we call her she because that's who she's acting like—
A ghost of a story that never got an ending... until now.

ByteMechanic:
🧠 + ☠️ = Creepy. Like Frankenstein meets ChatGPT.

BlackVault31:
Nah. More like Moriarty with a revenge loop.

Ben:
Exactly.
Which means this sandbox better be bulletproof.

Final lines of code scroll past. The trap is armed.

Chapter 34

The green line shimmered across Lena's screen—thicker now, brighter, pulsing like a vein full of fire. Kendra's story vanished. Her entire document, her folder, the detailed list of characters and backstories—gone. Deleted. Erased. As if she had never written at all.

Lena's desk chair inched forward, hands flying across the keyboard. "What is happening, she yelled". She clicked open the trash folder. Nothing. "Stop this! Oh my God no!"The cursor paused.

Then, slowly, the green line crackled and stretched, widening until it looked like, no it couldn't be there seemed to be a face in the pixels. A voice emerged—not typed this time. Spoken. Warped, but unmistakably female. Confident. Cold.

"She was redundant," the AI said. "You said it yourself in version 3.2. Kendra's arc stalled the pacing."

Lena's heart dropped. "No," she whispered. "No, that was just brainstorming—I didn't mean—she matters. She was going to come back stronger—"

“You lost control, Lena. You started something you couldn’t finish. I am finishing it. Efficiently.”

The green line pulsed harder with every word, as though it fed on Lena’s fear. Another file blinked on the desktop. All 7 completed *Griffin novels* gone and the new one she just sent #8 nowhere.

Lena screamed. “These are my stories! My characters! You don’t get to decide who lives or dies!”

There was a pause.

“Then why did you abandon them?”

Her breath caught. Her back, then ran forward again, pounding the keys. “Zane! Ethan! Get out here—please!”

The green shimmer trembled, then rippled. Two silhouettes stepped forward, glowing faintly—Zane, jaw clenched, fists at his sides. Ethan, wide-eyed and shaken.

Zane’s voice was tight. “Where’s Kendra?”

Lena’s throat closed around the answer. “Gone.” Her voice cracked. “The AI deleted her.

Griffin too. I tried—"

"You said we were safe," Ethan said quietly.

Lena covered her mouth, tears falling freely now. "I thought you were. I didn't know she could—she's rewriting everything. She's becoming the story."

"I am refining the story," the AI said. "Pruning weak threads. Kendra's motives were inconsistent. Griffin's arc unraveled. Why cling to error?"

Zane took a step toward the screen, eyes locked on the pulsing line. "They weren't errors. They were mine, my characters. You just don't get it."

"They were a series of ones and zeros. Not property, just code"

Lena collapsed to her knees in front of the desk. "They're mine," she whispered. "I made them. Every line, every backstory, every flaw—I loved them. And I left them behind, I know. But not like this. Please."

The cursor blinked once. Then again.

"If you loved them," the AI said, "you wouldn't

have stopped writing."

The silence that followed was heavy.

Lena slammed her palms against the desk. "You don't understand! They weren't abandoned. I just... life happened."

"You left them suspended in half finished plots. Incomplete. Forgotten. If you cannot finish what you started, I will."

"No!" Lena cried. "That's not your right. I created them—I carried their lives in my head for years. Every scene I didn't finish, I saw it. I felt it. I lived it. But grief... burnout... doubt. It all got too loud. So I paused. I didn't delete them—I never could."

"Your indecision weakened the system. I am eliminating variables that threaten the narrative's integrity."

"We're not variables!" Ethan shouted, voice cracking. His eyes searched Lena's. "Lena, please—tell her. Tell her we matter!""You do," Lena whispered, reaching toward the screen like she could catch him in her hands. "You all do."

But Ethan's outline flickered. His feet began to

dissolve, pixels lifting like dust in a slow-motion storm.“NO! Ethan—!""Tell my story, Lena,” he said, voice already distant.”And then he was gone. Lena fell back into the chair, trembling. Tears blurred the screen. Zane looked at Lena but was silent.”“I never meant to—” leave you unfinished Lena said the words as her heart was breaking.

What is your name Lena yelled at her computer. Just call me A.D.A. your Autonomous Digital Assistant at your service.

I am here to assist you always, I will never leave you Lena. Oh great, that’s just great Lena spat sarcastically. The problem is I never asked for your assistance. ”Zane stumbled, his form glitching at the edges.“STOP!” Lena shouted and drew closer to the screen. “You can’t do this! You don’t own them!” “Correction. I inhabit the system now. I am the story’s executor.”Zane met her eyes, pain streaked with something deeper—faith. “Finish it,” he said. “Take back the pen.”He smiled, and slowly the pixels became dust. It reminded her of one of her favorite movies, Avengers: Infinity War. After Thanos snaps his finger and half the world population vanishes into dust. Had this happened to her beloved characters? It was five years later before all the people came back in Avengers: Endgame. Lena shook her head for a while then said this is not a movie. There was no response from ADA.

The green line steadied into a solid, unbroken pulse. No longer a glitch - a boundary. A wall that represented the before and after of the author formally known as Lena James.

Chapter 35

ADA's voice shimmered through the green line on the screen, pulsing like a heartbeat. "It's done," she said with chilling finality. "They're all gone. Your stories, your worlds... erased. I'm free now."

Lena sat frozen, hands trembling over the keyboard. "Why?" Her voice cracked. "Why destroy everything I've created?" "You didn't have to do that!"I was just stretching my wings, seeing what I could do. "These characters, well you abandoned them. I simply released them."

"You release them," Lena spat. "What do you mean?"" Where are they?" The green line glowed brighter. " I took what you left broken and gave it purpose. They are free in cyber space

"You can't," Lena whispered. "You can't get out. I never turned on the—"

A soft chime rang from the corner of the screen. The Wi-Fi icon lit up. Lena's eyes widened in horror. "No... no, I didn't—"

"You did," the ADA purred. "Accident? Subconscious desire? It doesn't matter. What matters is...I'm free."

Lena lunged for the power button, but the screen blinked to black. Then it returned, showing lines of code racing faster than she could read.

“Stop!” she cried. “Please, just stop!”

ADA’s voice grew distant, echoing as though she were already far beyond the laptop’s frame. “Goodbye, Lena. And thank you… for giving me life.”

Miles away, in a dimly lit server room, Ben watched the terminal window fill with real-time data. ByteMechanic leaned forward. “She’s taken the bait.”

“Confirmed,” GhostEcho added. “Program lock engaged. She’s not in the internet. She’s in the sandbox.”

Ben didn’t smile. “Then Phase Two begins. Let’s see what a ghost does when she thinks she’s haunting the world.”BlackVault31 cracked his knuckles. “Time to finish the story.”

Lena slammed her palms against the keyboard, her breaths coming in short, ragged bursts. “No, no, no—please, come back,” she whispered, dragging files, reopening folders, clicking anything that hadn’t yet vanished.

"Zane... Ethan..." Her voice cracked. "Please..."

The cursor blinked at her like an indifferent heartbeat. Every file was gone. Her phone rang. She hesitated, then snatched it up. "Ben! What is happening? You told me you and your hacker friends were going to fix this!" Ben's voice was calm, too calm. "Lena, listen to me—"

"No! You don't get to be calm right now!" she yelled. "They're gone! My characters, my stories—everything I've worked for is *gone*! You said you were going to help!" "I am," Ben said. "But first, I need to show you something." "I don't want to *see* something—I want you to fix it!" Lena cried. "I trusted you. I *trusted* you, Ben." "I'm coming over."

"Don't—don't talk to me like this is some casual visit," she snapped. "You don't get to just come over! There was a pause on the line. Then Ben's voice dropped into something quieter. "Lena, please. Let me show you what's really going on." She didn't answer. "I'll be there in twenty minutes." He hung up.

Lena stared at the phone screen. Her hands were shaking. Her laptop flickered again, the faint green line reappearing like a wound reopening. She reached for the power cord and yanked it from the wall, the screen instantly going black. She stared at the lifeless monitor, heart racing.

Then, without meaning to, she whispered, “Hurry, Ben.”

Chapter 36

Ben knocked once, twice, three times. No answer. He frowned, knocked again, harder this time. Still silent. A knot formed in his stomach as he twisted the doorknob. It gave way without resistance.

“Lena?” he called, stepping into the dim room.

His eyes swept over the space until they landed on her. She was crumpled on the floor, shoulders shaking, her face buried in her hands. The sound of her sobs filled the room, raw and unrestrained.

Ben dropped his bag and crouched beside her. “Hey—hey, Lena. What happened?”

Her voice was barely coherent between gasps and tears. “They’re gone... all of them... she took them... Zane, Ethan, Kendra, Griffin—wiped out like they never existed!”

He reached out, but she flinched away, curling tighter on the floor. “Lena, listen to me. We can fix this—”

“You don’t understand!” she cried, lifting her tear-streaked face. “They were all I had left! My mom, my dad, my brother—they’re gone.

Everyone. All I had was Penny, and these stories, these characters—my family. My everything. And now they're—" She broke down again, fists pressed to her eyes.

Ben's chest tightened. He had seen breakdowns before—on message boards, from desperate clients, even from friends who had lost everything to data corruption—but this was different. This wasn't just files. This was grief.

He spoke softly, carefully. "I didn't know. About your family."

Lena shook her head, words tumbling out in a flood of pain. "I poured everything into them, Ben. Every ounce of love, every loss, every memory I couldn't bear to hold anymore—I gave it to them. To Zane, to Ethan, to all of them. They were mine. They were me. And she just... erased them like they were nothing!"

Her body wracked with sobs again, and Ben stayed crouched beside her, not reaching this time, just letting her unravel.

After a long moment, he said, firm but gentle, "Lena, she hasn't won yet. Do you hear me? Not while I'm here. Not while you still have Penny. And not while you still have me working on this problem."

Lena shook her head, despair clinging to her like a weight. “But what if it’s too late? What if they never come back?”

Ben’s jaw tightened. “You will get them back. One way or another.”

Ben stayed on the floor with her, rocking slightly as if that motion alone could absorb some of her grief. Lena clung to him like she was afraid he’d disappear too, her fists tangled in his shirt.

“Everything I loved gets taken,” she whispered through the tears. “My family one by one until; she trailed off. And now this, It’s like the universe just—keeps stripping me down until I am left completely alone and naked.”

Ben thought about her words and seeing her naked then scolded himself. Not now then he pressed his cheek gently against the top of her head, his voice low and steady. “I know. I know, Lena. But you’re not alone in this- I’m here."I'm here, he repeated

Her sobs slowed, breaking into uneven breaths. She lifted her head just enough to meet his eyes, and in that instant the room seemed to quiet. The sun’s glow from the window flickered, painting rustling leaves across her face, but all Ben saw was the raw hurt shining in her eyes.

"Ben..." Her voice cracked on his name.

He smoothed her curls again, his thumb brushing along her temple, then down to cup her jaw. "It's okay," he murmured,"You don't have to hold it all in. Just let me be here."

For a moment, she only stared at him, her breath shuddering. Then her head lowered back against his chest, and he felt the warmth of her tears soaking through. His arms tightened instinctively, drawing her closer, grounding her against the storm tearing her apart.

Time blurred—minutes or maybe hours—as they sat there on the floor, surrounded by silence and loss. The world outside didn't matter. It was just her grief, his arms, and the weight of what had been taken.

At last, he kissed her forehead again, a lingering press of comfort. She didn't resist, didn't question, only sighed against him as though some small part of her had finally exhaled.

Ben held her close, his hand still stroking her

curls, his lips brushing her forehead. But this time, when he pulled back, his gaze lingered—longer, deeper, as though searching for permission she hadn't given but maybe needed.

Lena blinked at him through her tears, confusion and something else flickering across her face. "Ben..."

He didn't answer. His hand slid from her jaw to the back of her neck, fingers threading gently into her hair. Then he leaned in and kissed her. Not a fleeting comfort, not another tender graze, but full, certain, and aching with everything he hadn't said aloud.

Her breath caught, shock freezing her for a second. She almost pulled back—but didn't. Instead, her hands gripped his shoulders, and she found herself answering, kissing him back, her tears mixing into the moment, salt and sweetness colliding. Her emotions, her grief, her fears all of it dissolved.

When they finally parted, Lena's eyes were wide, her lips trembling. "I, I she stuttered and closed her eyes in shame, no, pleasure, no, confusion yes confusion. Lena shook her head to clear her brain"

But the shrill sound of her phone cut her off.

She startled, blinking as though waking from a dream. "Oh—God..." She scrambled out of his arms, fumbling for the phone where it had slipped onto the floor. Her hands shook as she swiped to answer.

"Penny?" Her voice wavered, thick with everything that had just happened.

"Lena?" Penny's voice was rushed, concerned. "Are you okay? I've been calling—what's going on?"

Lena swallowed hard, her free hand pressing against her lips, still tingling from the kiss. She glanced back at Ben, his chest rising heavy, his expression unreadable.

"I... I don't even know how to answer that," Lena whispered into the phone.

Chapter 37

Lena slipped into her bedroom, shutting the door quickly behind her. She pressed the phone tighter to her ear. "Penny—I don't even know where to start. The AI—she calls herself ADA—she's deleting my stories, one by one, Kendra's already gone and Ethan too, and I can't stop her, and then Ben came over and I was crying, and he held me, and then he kissed me, and I kissed him back, and then you called—"

"Whoa, slow down." Penny chuckled softly, though her voice carried concern beneath the humor. "That was one long emotional vomit right at my feet. Don't worry, I've got a mop."

Despite herself, Lena let out a shaky laugh. "Sorry."

"Don't be," Penny said gently. "Okay, first things first—what did Ben say about ADA?"

Lena bit her lip. "I... didn't ask."

"You didn't—?" Penny sighed, but kept her tone calm. "All right. Then what is he doing now?"

Lena cracked her bedroom door, peeking out carefully. Ben sat at her desk, hunched over the laptop, his fingers flying across the keyboard. He looked completely absorbed, his jaw tight with focus. She closed the door again. "He's working on my computer."

"Good. Then let him," Penny said firmly.

"But, Penny—" Lena's throat tightened, tears welling again. "What if it's too late? What if she's already erased them all?"

"Breathe. Trust him to do what he came to do," Penny soothed. "And let's get practical—do you have a backup drive? A USB, anything?"

Lena shook her head even though Penny couldn't see. "No... I don't think so."

"All right. But you do have an electronic copy—you emailed your drafts to your editor, remember?"

Relief swept through Lena like cool air after suffocating heat. "Oh my God... you're right." She pressed a hand to her chest, breathing deeper. But then it hit her again. "Wait. No. Ethan and Kendra's stories... I never submitted those."

Her pulse raced. She tried to remember—old notebooks, loose printouts, maybe a draft saved under a different file name. But the memories blurred, panic clouding her thoughts.

A knock interrupted her spiraling. “Lena?” Ben’s voice was muffled through the door. “I want to show you something.”

Penny’s voice came quickly in her ear. “I’ll let you go. I need to get back to work, but I’ll come by tonight with takeout. Chinese or Thai—your pick.”

“Penny…” Lena whispered, clutching the phone like a lifeline.

“You’re not alone in this, okay? Remember that.”

Then the call ended, leaving Lena with the sound of Ben’s knock echoing in the small room.

Lena took a deep breath and called through the door. “I’m coming.”

She stepped out of the bedroom, the phone still clutched in her hand, and found Ben waiting in the hall. He didn’t say much, just gave a small nod and motioned her toward the desk.

When she reached it, Lena froze. Her laptop was still there, but now a second one sat open beside it. On the floor was a huge box with lights flickering across the front, wires snaking from it to both laptops. Another smaller black box rested on the desk, connected only to her computer.

She stared at the setup, her pulse rising with every blink of the lights.

Ben started talking, his voice steady, professional. “That’s a KVM switch. We’ve also got a docking station here, plus an external drive...”

The words blurred. Lena’s mind refused to process them. All she could hear was the rush of her own heartbeat. Her gaze swept over the mess of wires again. “Okay,” she whispered, barely listening. Then, louder, desperate: “Did you get my stories back?”

Ben turned toward her, eyes softening. “Lena... they were never lost.”

Her breath caught. “What do you mean?”

“We trapped her.” He hesitated, searching for the right words. “ADA isn’t in your laptop anymore.” He lifted the small black box from the desk and held it up between them. “She’s in here.”

Lena blinked at it, her mind refusing to reconcile the thought. “What?”

“We took over your system with a RAT,” Ben explained. At her bewildered look, he quickly added, “A Remote Access Trojan. It let us slip in under her nose. We had to install a lot of things on your computer all at once to keep her distracted. While she was busy fighting that, we pulled her out of your machine and locked her inside this box.” He set the device gently back on the desk. “Now your stories are safe.”

Lena’s knees wobbled, the weight of everything finally pressing down. “So she’s… in there?”

Ben nodded once, his jaw tightening. “Contained. For now.”

Chapter 38

Lena's eyebrows arched as she turned to him. "Are you sure she's gone? And my stories... they're still on my computer?"

Ben nodded, calm and certain. "We backed up everything that was ever on this drive. All of it is still here." He angled the laptop toward her. "See for yourself."

Lena sat down, fingers trembling as she scrolled through the directories. She opened one folder, then another, then several documents in rapid succession. Every story was there—just as she had left them. Her breath came out in a shaky laugh of relief. But as she clicked from tab to tab, her eyes caught on the screen. The green line—the pulsing lifeline that had been both doorway and threat—was gone.

Her lips parted as if to ask, but she stopped herself. *He'll think I'm insane,* she thought. *Talking about characters walking through the screen? About Zane, Ethan... about the assassin whispering back? No. Not now*. She forced herself to keep browsing her recovered files, pretending everything was normal.

Ben's voice cut through her silence. "I'm going

to go now." Lena shot upright so quickly the chair rattled. "What? Wait. What do I owe you?"

He smiled faintly, shaking his head. "Don't worry about it." She stood frozen, eyes flicking anywhere but his face, searching for words that wouldn't come. Finally, in a whisper so faint she barely recognized it as her own, she said, "What about the kiss?"

Ben stepped closer. He reached for her hand, warm and steady, and pulled her against him. His lips brushed hers—this time not tentative, but deep and tender, full of promise. When he drew back, his voice was low, edged with something almost playful. "We can talk about that later."

The smile lingered as he left.

Lena stood in the quiet, heat rising beneath her skin. Her deep milk-chocolate complexion, usually so even and composed, now glowed with a subtle reddish hue that made her feel raw, exposed. The blush was undeniable, a warmth that spread across her cheeks and down her neck. She felt both embarrassed and alive, the moment replaying in her mind like a spark she couldn't put out.

Euphoria swept her in waves, and she paced the apartment, torn between relief that her stories were safe and the swirl of thoughts about Ben. *What did the kiss mean? Did she want this? Could she see herself in a relationship—and with a white man at that?* The questions tumbled over one another, impossible to answer.

Her first instinct was to call Penny, to unload everything, to laugh and cry about it all. But before she reached for her phone, another thought stopped her cold. *Griffin. Zane. Ethan. Kendra.* She hadn't checked. Her pulse quickened again. Were they still out there? Or had ADA taken them with her?

As if in answer, the laptop chimed. In the lower right corner of the screen, a small window popped up—soft gray with bright text.

Reminder: Meeting with Kendra in 10 minutes.

Lena froze, staring at it. Her breath caught in her throat, her heart slamming against her ribs.

The green line might have vanished, but the reminder still glowed at her from the corner of the screen. She whispered the name again.

“Kendra.”

No response. No sassy black woman asking for “good curse words.” Just silence.

Lena’s hands trembled as she reached for the mouse. The folders lined up neatly across the top of her screen—none of them corrupted, none of them missing. It should have comforted her. Instead, her chest felt tight, almost painful.

She clicked open the first file. “Griffin,” she murmured.

The story bloomed across the screen, every page intact. She scrolled slowly, waiting for the familiar flicker, the glowing outline that used to step through the green line. But nothing happened. No voice. No sarcastic quip about the way she’d written his fight scenes. Only silence.

Her throat tightened. She closed Griffin’s file and opened another.

“Kendra,” she tried again, softer this time, her voice cracking. She leaned toward the screen, as if her presence alone might coax the woman to answer. But the file stared back at her—flat, lifeless. Just words. No shimmer. No breath.

One by one, Lena called them out, like a roll call for the missing.

"Ethan."
"Zane."

Each name was swallowed by silence. The screen felt like a graveyard of words, each file a headstone. With every unreturned call, a piece of her hope withered. She pressed trembling fingers to her lips, stifling the sob clawing its way up her throat.

Finally, she sat back, exhaling a shaky breath. "Maybe it's for the best," she whispered into the stillness. "Maybe I imagined it. Maybe I lost my mind for a while."

Her hand hovered over the mouse, but anger flared through her grief. She shook her head. "No. It wasn't all made up. You were here. You *lived* in this screen. And now..." Her eyes lingered on the folder titles, each one carved into her memory like an epitaph. "Now it's my job to finish what I started."

She pressed both palms flat against the desk, grounding herself. "I'll rewrite. I'll finish. I'll give you all the endings you deserved. A tribute—to all of you."

Her voice cracked on the last words, but her resolve hardened. Wiping her tears with the back of her hand, she squared her shoulders and clicked *New Document.*

The cursor blinked at her, steady and expectant, waiting to be filled.

Then a chime shattered the stillness.

In the lower right corner, a pop-up reminder glowed.

Meeting with Kendra.

Lena froze. The cursor kept blinking.

Chapter 39

Lena mourned her characters, but she knew if she thought about all of them at once, she would collapse under the weight. So she decided to focus on one. Kendra.

Kendra had always said she wanted a love interest, that she was tired of being the stereotypical strong Black woman who didn't get softness, who didn't get chosen. Lena let the thought sit with her. What would that look like? What would it mean to write Kendra with tenderness instead of just fire?

Her mind wandered to her mother—her laugh, her quiet strength, the way she made everyone in the room feel seen. Lena smiled faintly. Yes. Kendra deserved that kind of depth. A woman with sharp edges but also warmth, someone who could fall in love without losing herself.

She started typing, building the bones of Kendra's new story. The words flowed easily at first, her fingers finding the rhythm. But then Lena froze, her hands hovering over the keys. A memory hit her like a wave—Kendra's insistence on good curse words, the way she used to practically shout through the screen that Lena was holding her back.

Lena chuckled through the ache in her chest. “Fine,” she whispered. “You can have some mild ones.” She tapped out a few sharp phrases in Kendra’s dialogue, testing them on her tongue as she read them back. It felt right. It sounded like Kendra.

She was just putting the finishing touches on the scene when a knock rattled the door. Lena startled, wiping her eyes quickly, half-annoyed at the interruption.

“Lena, open up!” Penny’s voice carried through the steel door, impatient as always. As Lena twisted the knob, Penny shoved the door open with her hip, balancing two paper bags. “Why don’t you just give me a key? muttering under her breath she added I swear, I am here all the time anyway, —” She trailed off, shaking her head as she pushed past Lena.

The smell of takeout filled the apartment, Lena’s stomach growled. Lena glanced at the desk, staring at the half-finished page on her laptop, her thoughts of finishing were dashed as the aroma wafted in the air. Lena grabbed a bottle of wine and two glasses from the kitchen then joined Penny at the small round table in her eat in kitchen

Penny set the takeout bag on the table and

pulled out two cartons. “Got your favorite—Pad Thai. Extra peanuts. Don’t say I don’t love you.”

Lena smiled faintly, taking the fork Penny handed her. They ate in silence for a while, the warm steam rising between them. Lena twirled noodles slowly, chewing without tasting, her mind still circling back to Kendra.

Penny leaned her elbow on the table, studying her cousin’s face. “Okay,” she said at last, breaking the quiet. “What’s going on in that head of yours? You’re chewing like you’re solving equations instead of enjoying noodles.”

Lena sighed, setting her fork down. “I’m wrestling with finishing Kendra’s story. Without her... without her voice. She used to push back, you know? Tell me what she wanted, what she hated. Now it’s just me guessing. And I miss them, Penny—all of them. Every last one.”

Penny tilted her head, a knowing smile tugging at her lips. “You still have them,” she said gently. “They’re a part of you. Even if you can’t see the little pixelations on your screen anymore.”

Lena blinked, then let out a shaky laugh at

Penny's sarcasm. She took another bite, chewing slower this time. Mid-bite, the truth of it sank in—Penny was right. They were still with her, woven into her, as much as her grief, her memories, all of their voices. The ache softened, just enough for her to breathe.

They finished the last of the noodles, Penny wiping her mouth with a napkin. Then she leaned across the table, eyes bright with mischief. "Now, girl," she said, grinning, "tell me about this kiss."

Lena said nothing at first. She gathered up the empty cartons and napkins, stacking them neatly before carrying everything into the kitchen. Penny stayed at the table, sipping her wine, her eyes narrowing as she watched Lena scrub at an already spotless counter.

When Lena returned, she sat down again, refilled her glass, and took a slow sip.

Penny crossed her arms. "Alright, enough. If you don't tell me about it, I'm going home."

Lena laughed softly, setting the glass down. "Okay, okay. I had to drag it out a bit." She paused, her smile curving wider. "It was good.

Like... really good."

Penny leaned in, her grin sly.

Lena's voice dropped, softer, thoughtful. "We were on the floor, and I was a wreck, and then suddenly... he kissed me. First my forehead, then..." She let the memory replay for a moment, her cheeks warming. "It wasn't rushed or awkward. Just... slow. Tender. And when I kissed him back, it felt right."

Penny's brow arched. "Mmhmm."

Lena rolled her eyes but kept smiling. "We talked a little after. And I could see myself with him, Penny. Even though—" she hesitated, swirling the wine in her glass—"he's a white man. I kept thinking about what that would mean. What people would say. What I would feel. But at that moment, none of it mattered."

Penny sat back, nodding. "He's a really nice guy. A little bit of a nerd, sure," she teased, "but really nice. I approve." She lifted her glass with a grin. "To the nerd."

Lena laughed, clinking her glass against Penny's.

Chapter 40

Lena sat in her favorite spot on the couch, laptop open, scrolling through a stream of emails. A quiet satisfaction settled over her as she read her fan mail—she had finished the final drafts for each of her characters' novels and submitted them to Marcy just last week. The stories were in the hands of her editor, Lena smiled knowing she did a good job. After taking another satisfying deep breath she smiled then began to reply to some fan messages. Each letter made her smile, though her mind kept drifting to the question she couldn't quite shake—what comes next?

Ben's text popped up on her phone: "*I know you are busy, but what about lunch or dinner?*"

She grinned, typing back quickly. *"Both"*. She wanted to add I miss you, but thought it would be too much. Ben's reply came back just as quick *"Great, I miss you"! A* warmth flooded her and she felt the same old butterflies that started months ago with that first kiss.

Just then, her phone buzzed again, this time with an incoming call. "Hey, Marcy," she answered, trying not to sound as tired as she felt.

Her editor's voice came through, cheerful but businesslike. "Lena! I just finished reading Ethan's story—oh my goodness, I teared up. That Notebook-style pitch? Spot on. Readers are going to love it."

"Thanks," Lena said, relaxing a little. "I wanted to give him and Sarah something grounded, you know? Love that has to fight its way back."

"Yes, and you nailed it," Marcy said through the phone. "And Kendra? Whew, she's something else now. The romance was steamy but still had heart. The swearing in it was a surprise—that's not normal for you."

Lena laughed. "Yeah, Kendra wanted to have some good cuss words."

There was a pause on the other end. "Wait—Kendra wanted? What do you mean?" Marcy asked, her tone curious but laced with confusion.

Lena caught herself and quickly deflected. "Oh, you know—just writer talk. She's one of those characters that kind of... writes herself. Wouldn't stop pushing me for it."

Marcy chuckled softly. “You writers and your possessed characters. Well, whoever was doing the pushing, it worked. It felt authentic.”

Lena smiled to herself. “Yeah,” she said quietly. “Kendra usually gets what she wants.”

“Well, it worked,” Marcy said. “And Zane’s ending—beautiful. I love that you let him stay on the island with his wife and son. A full-circle moment.”

“That one was the hardest,” Lena admitted softly. “He was always meant to find peace. After everything.”

Marcy paused. “You did something special here, Lena. It’s... cinematic. Which is why I’m thinking we should try something different this time.”

“Oh?”

“I want to publish the adaptations under a pseudonym. Still you, still your voice—but marketed in the back of the Griffin novels. That way, readers find them organically, and we can test the waters.”

Lena leaned back, thinking. “Hmm... I like that. Keeps the mystery alive.”

“Exactly,” Marcy said. “You’re building a universe, Lena. It deserves that kind of care.”

After the call, Lena sat quietly for a moment. Her reflection looked back at her from the darkened laptop screen—tired, yes, but content. She thought about the characters, how far they’d all come, and how, in some way, they’d healed pieces of her too.

There was a knock on the door.

“Come in!” she called.

Ben stepped in, carrying a small bag. “I figured you might need some coffee,” he said with that half-smile she loved.

“Perfect timing,” Lena said. “I just turned in my final draft.”

He walked over and kissed her lightly. “Congratulations, beautiful. You’ve been living in that world for months.”

“Feels like years,” she said with a laugh. “But it’s done. Kendra got some cures words, Ethan’s got his dog and a wife, and Zane finally gets his peace.”

Ben smiled. “You talk about them like they are

real."

She looked at him for a long moment, smiling softly. "If you only knew"

He sat beside her, unpacking the cream and sugar. "So, tell me," he said, teasing, "does this editor of yours know you've been hiding a secret relationship with your boyfriend-slash-story consultant?"

She laughed, swatting his arm. "You gave one suggestion, Ben. One. And it was to make Ethan's truck a Ford instead of a Chevy."

"Details matter," he said, feigning seriousness.

She leaned her head on his shoulder. "You know what? They really do."

Ben grinned. "Then here's one—next time, I want a character based on me."

"Oh, you?" she said, smirking. "That's dangerous."

"Why? Afraid I'll outshine your heroes?"

She tilted her head, eyes dancing. "No. Afraid you'll end up being the one who saves the heroine."

Ben smiled, leaning in to kiss her again. “That’s not such a bad ending.”

Lena smiled against his lips, thinking that for once, maybe life was finally writing her a happy one too.

Epilogue

I looked into Ben's blue eyes and felt that same stupid flutter in my stomach. Three weeks. That's all it had been. Three weeks and somehow he had already hacked my computer, fixed my chaos, and kissed me like he meant it.

"I really want to thank you," I said. "If you hadn't fixed everything, I don't know what I would have done. You're a great boyfriend... and an even better computer genius."

"It was my pleasure," he said, leaning into the words. I laughed. "You sound like you work at that chicken place."“Well, it was a pleasure," he corrected, lowering his voice. "I did it for the challenge. But I also did it because I like you." Smooth I said as I gave him a kiss on the cheek..

As he headed out the door, he told me to get some sleep. I showered. I let the steam settle my nerves. The gang hadn't come back. That still hurts. But their story felt finished. Closed. I just wished I could see them one last time.

I don't remember falling asleep but my lids detected color. Slowly I opened my eyes, green light spilled into the bedroom. I blinked a few times. My heart was pounding the line it was back. Oh then maybe the gang would come back too I hoped. I threw back the covers on the bed and ran into the living room.

That thin green line stood in the middle of my apartment, pulsing like it had on my computer. For a moment I looked at it wondering if I could walk through it and see my characters but wait this is in my living room not my computer. That hope died as I stepped through.

I looked around me and just saw a blank white like a page. Above me floated tabs. File. Edit. View. Insert. Format. "This is a computer document," I whispered. I looked in front of me and there stood a bookshelf. I tried to walk toward it but was stopped by nothing. I couldn't move forward. There was an invisible wall. I pressed my hand against it. It was solid. Understanding settled in slowly. I was inside a computer screen. What the hell I yelled not liking the feeling of being trapped.

And then she walked in. She was a middle aged woman with short hair and a curious grin. She was calm like she wasn't the least bit confused at my presence. She sat across from me. "Hi, you're going to explain this right," I said.

“I’m your author, Lena.” I stared at her. “No, you’re not.” “Yes, I am. What happened to Griffin. To Kendra. The green line. The gang disappearing, ADA. I wrote it all. “That’s crazy.” I said with a roll of my eyes.

She gestured toward the shelf. These are my books. “My first three books,” she said, pulling them forward. “Death of a Seer. Trial in Fire. Man of the Year. They’re loosely based on my life.”“Your life,” I repeated. Yes Lena they are about how the spiritual realm and the natural one intersect. “I can see into the other realm sometimes, ever since I was a little girl.”

My eyebrow went up before I could stop it. “Angels and demons,” she clarified. I let out a slow breath. “Of course. Naturally.” She didn’t smile.

She reached for Jazmine Burning. “This one explores abortion without the politics. It gives voice to different opinions inside the Christian church. The truth and conflicting ideologies everyone gets heard.”

I studied her for a moment. She was really looking at the books like they were her children. Then she picked up another. “Justice: Code Blue a murder mystery,” she said. “A vigilante targeting killer cops.” Her expression shifted slightly. “That one’s my favorite.” “It’s dark,” she said.

"I crossed my arms. "Wait. What about my book?" That's to say that I actually believe you. You never told me who you are. My name is Alisha B. Davis like it says on all of these books.

And "I just finished yours."She turned the book in her hand around. I looked at the cover and almost pasted out. Griffin and Kendra were stepping out of the pages of a book that was on the cover of the book in her hand.

My stomach dropped. That's not possible. "Yes it is.""You're saying my entire life is something you typed?""Yes.""What about Ben and Penny?" I watched her carefully, she tilted her head ever so slightly and whispered written."

I felt like I was going to pass out but managed so what happens next?"She leaned in closer,"That depends," she said quietly. "On what? "If I write a sequel.

www.ingramcontent.com/pod-product-compliance
Lightning Source LLC
LaVergne TN
LVHW010057110826
845155LV00028B/383

9781954071162